DARE TO CHALLENGE

BARBARA RAE ROBINSON

Contact at barbararae@gmail.com

Cover design by Christy Keerins

Dare to Challenge / Barbara Rae Robinson

First edition

EBOOK ISBN: 978-0997182422

PRINT ISBN: 978-0997182439

❀ Created with Vellum

This book is dedicated to Rhay Christou, teacher extraordinaire. Her gentle guidance and love for my characters helped make this book what it is

CHAPTER 1

Sabrina Walters rounded the corner at a fast pace, her clogs clicking on the pavement. Kara Rasmussen was coming to pick up the earrings for her trip. Sabrina hated disappointing customers. That's not the way you stayed in business, yet stayed invisible.

Just past the furniture store, Sabrina stopped.

The door to her jewelry shop stood wide open.

Her heart rate soared, choking off her breath. She quickly scanned the area around the shop. No one seemed out of place. A woman across the street pushed a stroller. An elderly man walked by holding the leash of a small fuzzy dog. Both ignored her.

She looked back at the door. An icy shiver trickled down her spine. She'd locked that door when she'd left the night before. A small light had been burning. Now only dimness yawned from the interior. Was someone still inside?

The April breeze blew the door against a counter. She winced. But couldn't move.

A car door slammed.

She jumped and twisted around. "Kara." Panic elevated that one word.

"Is something wrong?"

"I locked this door last night." Her voice shook, but she couldn't help it.

"Are you afraid to go in?" Kara's tone was gentle.

"I guess I am." Her racing heart slowly eased its pounding, thanks to Kara coming on time. But her usual courage had vanished.

"I'll look around, to make sure there's no one inside." Kara flipped back the front of her light jacket and took a gun from a holster at her waist.

The sight of the gun jolted Sabrina, even though she knew Kara worked for a detective agency. The gun shouldn't have surprised her.

Kara disappeared into the shadows.

Sabrina shrugged out of her backpack and set it on the floor just inside the door, and glanced around. Kara had gone into the back room.

Something was wrong. She carefully stepped to the center of the showroom. And drew in a quick breath. Her liquid silver necklace sat on the floor off to one side, sparkling in a ray of sunlight coming through the window. "Kara." Another word wrapped in panic.

Kara came from the back room. "What is it?"

"That necklace over there." She pointed. "It was on the mannequin in the window when I left last night."

"There's no one here. But someone made a mess of your work table."

Sabrina grabbed her backpack and hurried into her workroom. All her gems and beads had been emptied out of their

2

plastic boxes and piled in the middle of the table, one particularly large amethyst at the peak. She dropped her backpack on a chair and looked for any other damage. A gum wrapper sat on the top of the trash basket. Spread out so she could clearly read the brand name.

A frisson of fear scuttled up her backbone. The scent of cinnamon in the air triggered alarming memories. The gum wrapper. The necklace on the floor. The mess on the table.

"This is bizarre." She rubbed at her forehead. No. It couldn't be Nathan. Not here. Not now.

"What aren't you telling me?" Kara stared straight at Sabrina and she couldn't keep from squirming.

"Nothing." She clutched her arms in front of her, to hide their shaking.

"I don't care how far-fetched it is. You're acting scared. If you have a hunch or a feeling, tell me. Let me decide if it's relevant."

"But you're a detective. You deal in facts." Even her voice was shaky.

"Sometimes cases are solved by hunches. Tell me."

Sabrina heaved a big sigh. "It is far-fetched. That gum wrapper on top of the trash." She pointed to it. "I don't know who put it there."

"Okay, let's suppose your intruder chews gum. What brand?"

"The same one my cousin, Nathan, always chewed."

"And?"

"Nathan used to hide my things and pile up my toys in funny ways."

"How long since you've seen Nathan?"

"Fifteen years."

Kara continued to stare at her. "Are you afraid of Nathan?"

3

"Yes." She didn't hesitate. It was the honest truth. She never wanted to see him again.

"Then we'd better call the police."

"What will they do? I don't think he took anything, just moved things around and left that gum wrapper where I'd see it." She took a quick tour of the work room and the showroom and didn't spot anything missing.

Kara followed her into the showroom. "You think he left that gum wrapper on purpose?"

"If it's Nathan, yes. He was a bully, always tormenting me. But why now? Why in Portland?"

"Where does he live?"

"He was in Riley, Oklahoma, the last time I saw him."

"Tell me more. Why does your intruder make you think of Nathan?" Kara leaned on the wooden edge of the showcase, her dark red hair shining in the sunlight from the doorway.

Sabrina fiddled with an amber necklace hanging on a rack. "If it is my cousin, he's looking for weird things to do to shake me up. Like he did when we were kids."

"So what did he do then?"

"He was mean. He took my dolls and stashed them all over the house, in cupboards in the kitchen, sometimes. That made my grandmother mad, but she got mad at me, not him. His standard line was, 'Granny, she's the one lying. She's always trying to get me in trouble.'"

"Did you both live with your grandmother?"

"No, he lived next door with his mother. I lived with my grandmother. In Riley, Oklahoma."

"Strange that he'd show up in Portland."

Kara followed her back to the workroom and sat at the table. "I'm betting that's how he got in." She jumped up and gave the window a push. It hung loose, leaving a gap big enough for someone to crawl through.

"I've told the landlord I want that window fixed, but he hasn't done it."

Kara sat at the table again. "Okay, we'll report this to the police as a breaking and entering, so it's in their records."

"What good will that do?" Sabrina sounded petulant, but she didn't care. She didn't trust the police to help her. The police didn't help a nobody.

"Not much, I agree. We don't know for sure it's Nathan." Kara sat back in her chair, her wry smile and the sparkle in her hazel eyes reminding Sabrina that Kara was above all else a detective.

"You came for your earrings." Sabrina bolted from her chair. "You're probably in a hurry and don't have time to waste talking about my problems." From the cabinet against the side wall, she took out a wrapped package.

"My flight to San Francisco isn't until mid-afternoon. I have all morning before I have to head to the airport." Kara unwrapped the package and held the three pair of earrings up to the light, one at a time. The greens and amber and gold tones sparkled. The colors were the same, but the designs and lengths varied. "Beautiful. Exactly what I wanted."

A flutter of pleasure soared through Sabrina. Kara always appreciated what she made for her. They went into the front of the store, to the cash register, and Kara paid with her credit card.

"Have a good trip. Don't worry about me. I'll call the police, not that it will do any good."

"My boss likes a good puzzle." Kara stopped at the door, her hand on the knob. "I bet he'd be willing to help you. I wish I didn't have to leave town today. I certainly would."

"You work for that detective agency. I don't have any money to pay for help."

"Sometimes Doug takes on cases because he wants to. He's the sole owner of Landreth Investigations. I firmly believe when he hears your story, he'll be eager to help. Don't worry about the money. He may charge you a token amount, but he can afford the loss."

Kara chuckled like it was an inside joke. "Lock up and let's go talk to him. You can tell him what you told me. And we'll report it to the police from there."

"I can't."

"Yes, you can. Let's see if our agency can help you figure out if it's Nathan. You do want to know for sure, don't you?"

"Yes, I do." A small flame of hope kindled inside her. Kara believed her. That softness in her eyes, that tone of voice. Maybe her boss could help.

She moved out from behind the counter. Portland was home now. She'd built a business she was proud of. She had true security for the first time in her life. She wanted to stay here forever, without fear.

A shudder rippled through her, settling in the pit of her stomach as a hard rock of dread.

Nathan.

If it was him, she'd have to run again.

~

"RAFE, ARE YOU HERE YET?" Doug's summons boomed over the intercom. "Come to my office." His vacation's-over tone held a touch of let's-get-down-to-business tossed in.

Rafe's stomach churned, an antsy, unsettled sensation. His two weeks away hadn't erased his self-doubt, his feelings of failure. He'd returned to New York, to the scene of his greatest failure.

He stood and picked up his cup of coffee. In this agency, you didn't keep the boss waiting.

When Rafe reached Doug's office, he stopped in the doorway. Doug stood in front of his desk, leaning on his cane. His confrontational stance.

"Did you sort out what was bothering you, while you were in New York?" No greeting. No pleasantries. Direct and to the point. Doug's way.

"I hope so." That was as positive as Rafe could own up to. He couldn't lie and say everything was okay. Or admit he still had some doubts. Doug knew why he'd left New York in a hurry two years earlier.

Doug limped around his desk and dropped into his chair. Once seated, he looked like any other dynamic big man. Lean and muscular, dressed casually in slacks and T-shirt. His ever present leather jacket hung on the coat rack in the corner.

Rafe settled into one of the two chairs in front of the desk and put his coffee cup on the coaster near the edge of the desk.

Doug stared at him, waiting.

"I saw Bethany's grave. Her parents put up a nice headstone. Even has an angel on it for our unborn daughter."

Doug's raised eyebrows spurred him to continue. "I went to see the guys at the precinct where I used to work. No one blames me for leaving like I did."

"For running."

"For running. The story of my life. But I'm through running. I'm not that scared fifteen-year-old kid dodging bullets. Or the cop whose life imploded in front of him."

"I believe you. You've settled. You've analyzed. You've grown as a person, as a detective."

Coming from Doug, that was high praise. Rafe wasn't sure if he needed to say anything.

"Thanks." He settled for the simple word, sincerely uttered.

"So, can you put it all behind you? Or are you still working through the mental and emotional part?"

"Why? What kind of job do you have for me?" He answered with a question of his own, because he wasn't sure how he felt. Was he ready, finally, to fully commit to the life he was building here?

"Helping a young woman. Sabrina Walters. She's afraid her cousin has found her and is tormenting her like he did when they were kids. She hasn't seen him in fifteen years."

His gut twisted into a hard knot. Was this case a test? Was his job at risk? He wouldn't let Doug down. Or the woman.

"Personal protection?" Not something the agency usually took on.

"Yes. Kara brought her in. She feels Sabrina is in danger and wants us to help her."

Rafe raised a brow. "And you agree?"

"Yes. And I want you to set up surveillance to catch the guy in the act. He broke into her shop last night, didn't take anything, but moved things around. She's afraid he may come back."

"Is she afraid he may hurt her?" That knot in his gut twisted tighter. Another vulnerable woman.

Doug leaned back in his chair like he was trying to get more comfortable. "Yes. If it's that cousin. They have a past that goes beyond the moving of toys and such. But she wasn't ready to talk to me about it."

"And you think she might tell me? Why not one of the women?"

"Kara is leaving today for a job in San Francisco and Alison is in court this week, winding up her latest job."

"So, I'm the choice, instead of Scott or Dave." A statement, not a question.

Doug eased out of his chair and limped around to the front of the desk, stopping three feet from where Rafe sat. "You're the most business-like and organized person on the team. She'll benefit from your way of working. She's a quiet mouse type. Shy. She makes custom jewelry from beads and gemstones and sells it in her own shop across the river on Burnside."

Rafe hesitated. "Do you think she'll trust me?"

"You'll have to earn her trust. We always do when we work with clients."

A moment of panic seized him. "Maybe she shouldn't trust me."

Doug glared at him, that characteristic scowling frown of his securely in place. "Okay, you didn't finish processing what was bothering you. Will that keep you from working? From protecting other people?"

Rafe stood and took a deep breath, his decision made. "No. I won't let it." Conviction road the top edge of his voice. He wouldn't shirk his responsibilities on the job. He'd cage his anger and self-doubt. And not let another woman down.

"Good. I told her I'd send someone to her shop this morning. She lives around the corner, a couple of blocks from the shop. Doesn't drive. Doesn't want you to be seen coming in. Go around to the alley and knock on the back door."

"So she has some basic intelligence. Yet she's afraid."

"That's the way I see it. I believe her. The police aren't taking this seriously. Only took a report over the phone. No personal contact."

"If we find out something is going on, do we call in the police?"

"They'll assign a detective if they think there's probable cause." Doug limped back to his chair. "They should be on this from the beginning." His voice carried a knife-edge sharpness.

"What's the name of the shop?" Rafe shifted his stance, ready to go to work. He could do this. The tightness in his gut eased.

"Designs from the Heart. Kara and Tricia both buy jewelry from her. The shop is small, but neat and clean. I checked it out earlier. Here's the address." He pushed a card across the desk.

Rafe picked up the card and glanced at it. "Any employees?"

"No. Sabrina works completely by herself and doesn't appear to have much money. I'm charging her a small amount, so she has a definite connection to our agency, but she gets our full support. We'll absorb the necessary expenses."

Rafe moved toward the door. Typical Doug behavior. It was usually the people without money who needed help the most. Doug would never get rich off his business. "I'll head over there now and see what needs to be done."

"I'd take this case myself if I could. This young woman is scared, and carries scars from her past."

Don't we all? Another twinge in his gut. The responsibility for another young woman was his.

Doug would watch from the sidelines. His crippled legs slowed him down, if speed was necessary. He'd have trouble defending someone being attacked.

"Damn that Moreno and his blasted bomb." Anger spiked Doug's words. He usually kept quiet about the past.

"You may get your chance at him someday."

"Sooner than I want to." More anger.

"What's happened I don't know about?" He moved closer to the desk again, his curiosity aroused.

"You knew Ramon Moreno was in Los Angeles again. Well, he's stronger than ever and still vowing revenge against me. He's coming north to finish me off, as soon as he feels it's safe to leave Los Angeles without jeopardizing the power base that he's rebuilt."

"A little man with a big ego. Do you still get information from Nick's contacts down there?"

"Yes. He has the same contacts as when he was a detective in L.A. I trust they're right. If you see anything suspicious, let me know immediately."

"Of course. We've got your back."

"One other thing. When we're away from the agency, I've authorized all of you to carry your weapons. You have concealed carry permits. And you update your skills regularly."

"So we're ready for Moreno when he arrives."

Doug frowned. "I wish I was a whole man. I wish I could meet Moreno on his turf. I wish I could kill the bastard."

"Sometimes the satisfaction kills something inside of you." His quiet words triggered a Taser-zap of guilt to his gut.

CHAPTER 2

*S*abrina hunched over her worktable in the back room of her shop. She added another amethyst gemstone to the necklace she was making, twisting the wire with her needle nose pliers, positioning it the right distance from the hematite stone next to it. Then she held the necklace up to the light. Her hands shook as she viewed the progress she'd made.

A large shadow passed by her workroom window.

Her chest constricted, tightening like a band around her heart. The detective was here. The one Mr. Landreth said would come. She had to let him in. She had to talk to him. She needed his help.

His knock rattled the back door.

She jumped out of her chair, opened the door a crack and peeked out. A big man. She pulled the door open fast, before she could change her mind.

"Sabrina Walters? I'm Rafe Campbell, from Landreth Investigations. May I come in?"

"Yes, come in please." She tried for a forceful voice, but it cracked. He stepped inside, filling the doorway. Dark hair. Dark eyes. A big man.

She stepped back, that band still tight around her heart.

"May I look around?" Polite, gentle words.

"Of course." She followed him as he toured the front of the shop and then returned to the workroom. She'd locked the front door and put up the closed sign so they wouldn't be interrupted.

"Not a large area for surveillance coverage. This ought to be easy." He smiled at her, seemingly a forced smile, like he was trying to put her at ease when he wasn't at ease himself.

A rather bizarre idea, but intriguing.

He looked down at her. "What did this guy do when he was inside the shop?"

She took a deep breath yet her jumping nerves wouldn't settle. "He must have come in through that back window that doesn't fit properly. I've told the landlord, but he hasn't fixed it."

"And all he's done is move things around?"

"And left a gum wrapper on top of the trash, smoothed out. The brand my cousin used to buy." It sounded weird even to her.

He poked around the frame of the window and scraped away some loose fragments of sill. "No wonder it was so easy for him to get in. This window won't stop anyone." He pushed it out, then pulled it back into place. "We'll have to leave it as is for now if we want to catch him in the act."

"I guess so." She hated the idea that Nathan, or whoever it was, might come back.

"I'll get the security firm that does our work to set up the surveillance equipment we need." He made a call on his cell phone, then turned to her. "It will take Paul a couple of hours to gather all the materials and get over here. Do you want me to stick around, or shall I come back later with him?"

"You can go. I'm okay. I'll open the shop and work on my jewelry." She rushed the words. She didn't want him sitting around here, watching her.

"All right." He stared at her, as if assessing whether he should leave her alone. Did she look that incapable? Maybe so. People took her for a weakling and took advantage of her. Especially the men.

"We'll come in through the alley. I'll knock on the door when we get here." He paired his words with another assessing stare.

She quickly crossed to the door and held it open. He left and she shut and locked the door. And the band around her heart gently eased. She didn't want to spend any more time than she had to with such an intimidating man. He overwhelmed her, made her feel small, and brought back feelings of helplessness.

RAFE ADJUSTED the camera in the corner, up near the ceiling, against a high cabinet. He aimed it toward Sabrina seated behind her work table. She was making a bracelet to match the necklace he'd seen her working on earlier. The same purple and black stones.

Doug was right. She acted vulnerable. But he'd need to attack that vulnerability to get answers to necessary questions. Questions that would help them help her.

"This camera will catch your intruder coming in the window." He descended the ladder. "And catch whatever he does with your things here on the table."

She glanced up at him. "Good." Then lowered her gaze to the bracelet and picked up another purple stone.

Paul, from the security company, finished adjusting the camera in the display area and came into the back room. "Ready."

"I'll turn the cameras on and test the feeds." Rafe powered up the laptop he'd left on the work table. Then sat in front of it.

Paul watched over his shoulder. "It ought to work fine. I've done hundreds of these installations."

Rafe chuckled. "I bet you have. Lots of break-ins these days." He wiped sweat off his brow with a handkerchief. The small shop didn't have an air conditioner and the day was too cool and windy to open the back window and the front door for air circulation. A typical April spring day in Oregon.

He hit several keys. "Ah ha. There's the image." The view of Sabrina came through clearly. Her wavy brown hair had fallen forward, shielding her face. She didn't raise her head. Somewhere under that full skirt and baggy sweater a frightened woman hid.

He glanced up from the laptop, at Sabrina across the table. Still hiding her face behind her hair. His task was to peel back the layers to reveal who she was, and where she came from. The information could help find whoever broke in and scared her enough that she stepped out of her comfort zone and accepted help.

Then he checked the image from the front of the shop. Anyone who came in the door would show up on the feed.

He glanced back at Sabrina. The sooner this job was over, the better. Something about Sabrina brought out his protective instincts. If he let his feelings get involved, he courted emotional suicide.

He'd do what he was trained to do. When the evidence was gathered, they'd turn this case over to the police and let them arrest the culprit. And this sensitive young woman could return to her normal life, which didn't seem normal to him. She was a puzzle. Trouble was, he liked puzzles as much as Doug did.

Hands off, buddy. He had to keep his distance. His life was messed up enough. He couldn't take on someone else's problems, except as a professional. Then get the hell out before he got in too deep.

"Looks like everything is working." Paul picked up the tool box he'd repacked. "See you on the next job." He went out the back door.

Rafe locked the door, put the laptop in the cupboard, then secured the deadbolt he'd installed to keep the equipment safe from any prowler.

Sabrina's head was still bent over her work table. She held the bracelet she was working on, added another purple bead to the strand of wire, then twisted the wire with needle nose pliers. The gems sparkled, even in the muted light from the overhead light bulb.

Information gathering time. Before he started feeling sorry for her for opening sensitive topics.

She must have sensed he was watching her. She looked up, meeting his gaze, then lifted her chin. Was that a conscious choice, to make herself seem less vulnerable? She struck him as intelligent and street smart. Like when she told him to use the back door.

"The cameras and sensors are ready. Only someone suspicious enough to look for them will be able to spot them."

"Good. I want him caught. I don't want to keep wondering what's going to happen next." She said the words with emphasis, but softly uttered. Like she wasn't used to speaking out for herself.

He sat in the chair across the table from her. Anyone else

and he would have moved around to her side of the table. But she flinched whenever he got close.

He pulled a notebook and pen from his pocket. "You told Doug about a cousin you had problems with in the past. That you think it might be him. Why?"

She dropped the purple bead in her hand and stared at his notebook. A shudder rippled through her shoulders and trembled her bottom lip. As much as he didn't want to cause her distress, they needed information only she could give them. He had a feeling that no one else knew why she was afraid of Nathan.

She pushed the beads away from her. "He used to move things of mine when we were kids. Hide them. Put them where my grandmother would find them and scold me."

"What else?"

A long hesitation. She was deciding how much to tell him. Why? He waited, kept his gaze on hers, yet tried not to intimidate her.

"He was mean and he hit me when we were alone together. I had to make sure we weren't alone."

"What's his name?"

"Nathan Prescott."

He wrote the name down and spelled it back to her. "Do you know his middle name? Where he was born?"

Her lips curved in the first hint of a smile he'd seen. "He hated his middle name. That's the only way I could get back at him. I called him Nathan Oswald Prescott when I was mad at him."

"I'd be mad too if someone called me that."

"But that's not why he picked on me." Her words were defiant, her green eyes sparked with specks of gold fire.

"Where was he born?" Rafe leaned back. Her subtle fragrance

teased his senses. Probably used lavender scented shampoo like what his mother had used. One positive thing he remembered about her short life. He willed away unpleasant memories.

"Riley, Oklahoma. It's a small town. I was born there too and lived there until I had to leave."

Had to leave. He'd come back to that statement. "And Nathan stayed there?"

"I guess so. He was still living at home with his mother the last time I saw him. No reason for him to leave. I was the one who had to go." He caught the bitterness in her tone. And the slight accent. She must have worked to get rid of it.

"His mother's name?"

"Jessica Prescott."

"How long since you've seen Nathan?"

"Fifteen years." She drew out the words until they threatened to snap.

She'd obviously kept track of the passing time. "Do you still have other family in that area?"

She pulled the plastic container of black beads in front of her and picked out two. "I don't know." She set the beads next to the unfinished bracelet.

"Who else was there?" Painstakingly slow, but progress. She was giving up a few details that would help his search. He glanced at his list.

"My grandmother. She raised me."

"Name?"

"Lila Fay Walters." She spelled it for him and he wrote it down.

"How is she related? Father's mother? Mother's mother?"

"My mother's mother. I never knew my father." Again, defiant words.

"What happened to your mother? Why did your grand-mother raise you?"

"She left when I was five."

"Her name?"

She hesitated. "Joanna Walters."

Ah, she was embarrassed. An unwed mother for a mother. And she didn't know her father. No wonder she was messed up. Who was he to talk? He'd known his old man, but that didn't help him. Almost got him killed.

"What are you going to do with this information?" Fear quaked her voice. Like she didn't want her privacy violated.

"When someone is being stalked..." He hesitated, giving her time to get used to that word. "We look at friends and family first. It's often someone the victim knows."

"That's what scares me."

He kept his expression neutral, though a smile threatened to break through. At least she was honest. "Why? Has anyone else hurt you?"

She took a deep breath and looked away. "My grandmother kicked me out."

"Why?"

"I got into trouble." She didn't look at him but at the bracelet and the containers of purple and black gemstones in front of her.

He doodled on his notepad, waiting. She fiddled with the gemstones, selected two purple ones and put them next to the half-finished bracelet.

She was better at dodging his questions than he'd given her credit for. He'd have to put Erik, the tech whiz at their agency, to work on her background. If the information was out there, Erik would find it.

One more try. "How old were you when you were kicked out?" His tone dared her to evade the question.

She drew in a big breath. Another hesitation move.

"Fifteen."

"Why? What kind of trouble? What are you holding back? What don't you want us to know about you?" He gentled his voice, trying to sneak past her defenses.

"Just find who broke in here." She shoved the trays of beads into the middle of her work table.

"Don't you want to know why he broke in?" More gentle words, softly spoken, to pry loose her secrets.

"How much jail time will he get?" She twisted a scarf that lay on the table.

"Maybe probation. Nothing was stolen. We need evidence he wants to harm you."

"Oh." Her eyes widened into a scared rabbit stare.

"So, think about everything that could help me find whoever it is and put him away for longer. We have to know this is more than a childhood prank." Her secrets ran deep. He'd dig again later.

"I'll think about it." She pushed at the necklace, clearing a space in front of her. A nervous gesture.

He picked up his pad and pen, put them into his pocket. "I'd like to see where you live. We might need to make security upgrades there, in case that's his next target."

Her sigh was long and drawn out, yet another hesitation move. "You're right. Okay, we can go out the back door and down the alley and around to my house without going out on Burnside."

"Good. He might be watching the front of the shop."

"You really do want him to come back." Her words accused.

He tried for a gentle tone. "He has to come back if we're going to catch him." She stiffened.

"What if he saw what's gone on here today?" That wide-eyed look returned.

"We had to take that chance." He stood. "Let's go."

"One minute. I have to grab my things."

She took a navy backpack from behind the table, shoved her laptop into it and the cell phone laying on the table. The backpack appeared to be stuffed. He'd like to know what else was in there. Was she prepared to run? He had a feeling there was a lot more to her story than she'd told him. Was she that scared?

CHAPTER 3

*S*abrina unlocked the front door to her house. Rafe was right behind her.

Her stomach churned. Too close. Too big.

She'd brought a man she'd just met to her house. She glanced back at him. He didn't have an intimidating look. And he was polite, not demanding.

Maybe he'd look around quickly and get out of here. Then she'd go back to the shop, and finish that necklace and bracelet set she'd promised a customer.

Rafe closed the front door and followed her into the living room. She dropped her backpack on the couch. "What do you want to see?"

He stood in the middle of the room and looked around. "First, tell me if anything is out of place. Can you tell if he was here?"

"In my house?" Her voice squeaked.

"If he knows where your shop is, he must know where you live."

"I hadn't thought of that." She glanced around the small space. Nothing had been moved. She went into the tiny kitchen. Nothing. "No, he hasn't been here. He makes it obvious." She returned to the living room.

"Good. Now we make sure he can't get in without disturbing the peace of the neighborhood."

"What do you mean?"

"If the doors are securely locked and the windows have good latches, he'd have to break glass to get in, or kick in a door."

Fear sliced through her. "Oh." Was he trying to scare her on purpose? She glared at him.

Rafe took out his notebook and pen, then started his inspection by checking the locks on the front door. His frown wasn't reassuring. She stood back and watched him work. He checked both windows in the living room, then went to the kitchen. She sat on the couch, to keep out of his way. The kitchen and utility room were both tiny. The whole house was small. Which suited her just fine. Less space to take care of.

Rafe returned to the living room. "We'll replace both locks on the front and back doors. They're all flimsy and easy to get past."

"Even the dead bolts?"

"Yes. They're cheaply made." He started toward the stairs. "Now the upstairs."

She followed him up, then stood in the hallway while he checked the two small bedrooms and the bathroom.

He came back to the hallway and stopped under the smoke detector. "Hard wired or battery?"

The smoke detector. The churning in her stomach intensified. He was thinking about a lot of things that hadn't occurred to her. "I don't know."

"You're renting?"

"Yes."

"I'll take a look, but I need a step stool to reach it."

"I have a chair." She reached around the corner into her bedroom and pulled a wooden chair into the hallway."

He frowned at her. "Nothing steadier?"

"No."

He put the chair against the wall and tested its strength with one foot. Then put his full weight on the chair and reached up. She held her breath. She didn't want him to hurt himself trying to help her.

He snapped off the cover and removed the unit from its holder. Wires hung from the ceiling. "Hard wired. If the electricity is cut off, the alarm won't work. We'll add a battery unit as backup." He replaced the unit and cover and stepped down.

"Are you worried about fire?" Her voice quaked, though she tried to keep it steady.

"A possibility. We don't know his plans. Or why he's here. Or if he intends to hurt you in some way." He moved the chair back into the bedroom and started down the stairs.

She followed him down to the living room. And glanced at her backpack still sitting on the couch. She was almost ready. A couple more things to cram in there. She wanted to stay in Portland, but if she had to go, she could. At a moment's notice. That's the way she'd lived her life since leaving Oklahoma.

"So what all did you find wrong with my house?" Her tone sounded defensive, even to her.

"Enough. The locks on both doors. The smoke detector. The window latches on the ground floor wouldn't keep anyone out."

That churning in her stomach returned. "I won't be able to sleep tonight."

"I'm your bodyguard. I'll protect you."

"Bodyguard? I don't need a bodyguard. You can't stay here." The words came out loud and panic filled.

"Do you really want to take your chances alone?"

"Yes."

"Okay, but I'll be back later to check on you."

"You can't stay here." Even more panic in her words this time.

"Right now I'm going to the agency, to report to Doug and get his okay on the upgrades I need to make. Go back to the shop if you want to. I'll see you later."

He went out the front door.

He said he'd be back. Her situation here in Portland was fast getting out of control. *I don't want to leave.* The plea came from deep inside her.

"DOUG, GOT A MINUTE?" Rafe stopped in the doorway of Doug's office. Doug was behind his desk, reading a report using the filtered sunlight streaming through the window to his left.

"Sure." He set down the papers and shifted in his chair. "What more do you need for Sabrina's safety?"

Rafe chuckled. "You knew I'd find something else that needed doing."

"I counted on it."

Rafe sat in the chair in front of the desk and leaned back. "Okay, for starters, that little old house she lives in. It's a rental. No more secure than the shop. I want the door locks, window latches, and dead bolts replaced. A battery-powered smoke detector installed upstairs and another downstairs. The one upstairs is hard-wired."

"Okay, that's easy to do. Cameras?"

"The house is tiny, two stories, on a narrow lot. Motion detectors tied to bright lights outside, both front and back would be more effective. That way no one can get close without being exposed. Might be enough to keep the guy away from the house."

"Good idea. But why? What more about her past have you learned?"

"Something has her spooked. She's afraid of Nathan but I don't think she's told me all that he's done to her. Her backpack is stuffed full. Looks like she's ready to run if something happens to scare her enough. Though I have the feeling she wants to stay. She has the shop and a good business. More than she's ever had in her life."

Doug shook his head and scrunched his eyes. His signature frustration mode. "That's why she agreed to let Kara bring her to me. She can't take everything with her in the backpack."

"Right."

"Do whatever you can so she can stay. That's a direct order." Typical Doug speak, in his authoritative voice.

"Okay. But why are you so concerned with keeping her here?" He had a hunch.

"She needs to be where she can be protected. Dani and Lindi are out there somewhere. And I can't find them. I've tried."

"Living under new identities?"

"I'm assuming Jenny changed their names when she fled to Nebraska with the girls. They were preschool age. Easy to do in those days." This time anger rode the edge of his voice. "When they left Nebraska, I lost track of them completely."

He'd heard the story about Jenny being harassed by Moreno. "Do you think there's any chance he'd go after the girls or Jenny now?"

"He might, now that he's back in Los Angeles. In retaliation.

Since I killed two of his sons in that raid." Doug gazed out the window. Took a deep breath.

Rafe waited.

Doug turned back. "We have to protect Sabrina in case that guy Nathan has more on his mind than mischief."

"I've worried about that too. I have four names for Erik to run. I gave them to him when I came in."

"Good. Who are they?"

"Her grandmother, Lila Faye Walters. She raised Sabrina. Her cousin, Nathan Prescott, the one she suspects. Nathan's mother, Jessica Prescott, and Sabrina's mother, Joanna Walters, who left when Sabrina was five."

"That's the entire family? No father?"

"She never knew her father. She did admit that her grand-mother kicked her out when she was fifteen, but she wouldn't tell me why. Said she got into trouble."

"Pregnant?"

"Probably."

"That's information you need. Make sure you get it. Right away." Doug's commander-in-chief voice.

"I told Sabrina I'd be back."

"Does someone else need to interview her?"

"Because I'm being too soft on her and not getting enough information?"

Doug leaned forward. "Why?"

Rafe frowned. "She's bringing out all my old protective instincts. I don't want to hurt her. Or cause her to get scared of me and run."

"You'll hurt her more by not getting the information that may end up saving her life. Think about that. This situation could go from annoying to dangerous."

"That's what I'm afraid of. I saw the fear in her eyes."

27

"I saw that fear too. So, do your job."

Rafe slumped in the chair. "Or I'll be replaced. I get it. I'll go to the house later, after I buy the things I need, and see what I can pry out of her."

The door opened and Nick Castellani poked his head in. "Meagan said I should come back."

"Come on in. Rafe and I have finished talking about the case. Though you may get this one before long. I have a hunch it's going to escalate."

"Oh, what do you have?" Nick pulled up a chair and sat.

"So far nothing but breaking and entering. The guy moved things around and spooked the woman who runs that little custom jewelry shop over on Burnside."

"Sabrina Walters? I've been to the shop with Tricia. She's been buying from Sabrina since the shop opened."

"That's the one. Do you know anything about her?"

"No. She's quiet. Like a little mouse who doesn't want to be noticed. Tricia says she talks more when I'm not with her."

"Let us know if Tricia has any insights into Sabrina's life that may help us."

"I'll talk to her."

"Is Tricia over her morning sickness?"

"No. She's staying close to home."

Doug stood and limped around to the front of the desk. "You take good care of my niece and grandniece or nephew."

"I can take care of Tricia." Nick laughed.

Rafe stood. "I'll go buy the locks and smoke alarms for the house and get Paul to do the outside work."

"Why her house?" Nick's voice indicated his interest.

"She thinks it's her cousin she hasn't seen in fifteen years who broke into the shop. He used to torment her when they were kids in Oklahoma."

"What do you think he's up to?"

"That's the big question. We don't have a motive. No robbery. Just harassment so far." Rafe outlined the events of the morning for Nick.

"She's scared. And afraid of this cousin." Doug's words were stern, almost angry.

Nick leaned forward in his chair. "Did she call the police?"

"The police took a statement over the phone." More angry words from Doug.

"Someone should have gone out and interviewed her. The department isn't that busy." Disgust oozed from Nick's tone.

Rafe edged toward the door. "I have a bad feeling about all this. She needs all the help she can get."

"I have a bad feeling about something else." Nick turned to Doug. "The word on the street gets more weird every day. Moreno is more ambitious than before he left for Mexico. We'd already heard he's not planning to stay in Los Angeles. That he's turning over that operation to a subordinate and moving north, to take over the northwest territories, including Portland."

"What else?" Doug asked.

"He's announced it publicly that he wants you in his cross hairs."

"Remember the message I got back in October. He went to Mexico to regroup and rebuild his organization after we busted things up in that raid. Now he's ready to carry on the feud with me."

"He's determined to kill you this time, Doug. You need to go on an extended vacation. A world tour." Rafe threw out the possibility, though he knew Doug wouldn't do it.

"No way." Predictable Doug.

"You might not be lucky enough to escape with your life next time Moreno decides to hit."

"I don't have a wife he can kill this time." Again, predictable Doug.

"But we don't want to lose you. That car bomb almost did the job five years ago." Nick added his plea.

"Yeah. Patti didn't have a chance. She was closer to the car."

Rafe's heart clenched. Bethany hadn't had a chance either. A look of understanding passed between them. They'd both lost wives to senseless violence.

"Take good care of Sabrina." Doug's glare and tone carried an ultimatum.

"I will." Rafe headed out the door. A young vulnerable woman needed his help and he had to figure out how to keep her safe. He couldn't fail.

CHAPTER 4

*S*abrina carefully spilled the contents of her backpack onto the faded bedspread. Here was everything she needed if she left in a hurry, displayed under the light of the single bulb hanging from the ceiling.

Sitting on the edge of the bed, she shoved her laptop aside and gathered her five jump drives. Every design she'd ever created. Her beautiful necklaces of mixed gemstones and beads, intricate earrings that sparkled in the light. All keeping her alive not only with the money they brought in, but the security of knowing she could support herself. She could create more beautiful pieces wherever she went.

She dropped the jump drives next to the spare set of tools that would help her get started somewhere else. She pushed the small camera next to the tools, the camera that recorded images to spark her creativity and images of her finished products. The cell phone. She'd replace it with one of those throw-away ones.

Then she opened the inner pack that held her toiletries bag and extra hairbrush. A change of clothes. Her usual underwear, skirt, blouse, and sweater. Six pair of her favorite earrings. No room for a jacket. She'd grab it and wear it.

Two items left, the most important. She picked up a blue velveteen bag that held her personal treasures, but resisted the temptation to look through them tonight. Time was precious. Through the soft cloth, she felt the hard outline of the blue stone her mother had left for her. The only thing she had of her mother's.

The last item was a small brown wallet. She hugged it to her chest. It held her stash of cash, her precious lifeline for starting over in a new town whenever she had to move quickly. She didn't want to leave Portland, but she would if she had to.

She'd been in this little house for five years. The longest she'd been in one place since leaving her grandmother's house at fifteen. Pregnant and rejected.

Despite the detective's help today, she had that gut-twisting feeling that things would get worse. If she left now, left no trail, she could disappear for years. No renting a house or apartment and signing up for utilities. That may have been what tripped her up this time. She didn't need much money to live if she didn't have a house. This time she'd be more careful and live on the fringes. She'd take her sleeping bag. And the bag with her small pup tent, if she had time to grab them. Maybe go south to a warmer, drier climate. Where she could live outdoors more comfortably.

She reached for the backpack, to put the wallet in it. A shadow moved against the wall. She screamed and scooted across the bed, dropping the wallet.

"It's okay. It's me. Rafe."

Her heart pounded in her chest. "It's not okay. How did you get in?" She practically screamed at him.

He leaned against the door jamb, instead of coming into the

room. "I knocked. Several times. You must not have heard me. I saw the light so I figured you were here. I had to make sure you were all right."

"Did you break the door down?"

"No. I used a credit card to spring the latch. The door has a very flimsy lock. I'll install the new locks tomorrow."

"A credit card?" Her feeling of safety plummeted further. Nathan could get inside the house if he wanted. If it was Nathan.

"Yes. This house is easy to break into, just like the shop."

"You can see I'm all right now. You can leave." Then silently prayed he would. She glanced at the contents of her backpack spread out on the bed, then looked at him.

"Will you keep running the rest of your life?"

"If I have to." She glanced at the satchel of jewelry on the small dresser. She'd be leaving so much behind this time.

"Doug wants to help you stop running."

"He doesn't have to. It's my life."

"No, he doesn't have to. But he's that kind of guy." He pushed away from the doorway, into the room, stopping midway.

She stared at him. Still too close. Too big. Too intimidating.

Yet she wanted to trust him. That's the funny thing. She wanted to trust this big man who'd done so much for her already today. And here she was, planning to run again.

"Please. Just go." She tried not to sound like she was begging.

"No. I'm not leaving until I've had time to convince you we can help."

"What does Mr. Landreth get out of this?"

"Doug. He's Doug to everyone. He gets satisfaction helping people who are in trouble. He's a former cop. So am I."

"Why would he help me if it's going to cost him money?"

"Like I said. He's that kind of guy. He has plenty of clients who can pay his full fees."

He let out a big sigh. "There's another reason. You might as well know."

She waited.

"Doug has two daughters he hasn't seen since they were very young. A powerful drug lord would kill them if he found them. For revenge. Doug will help any vulnerable young woman who's in danger." He emphasized those last words.

"Oh." She could understand that. "Thanks for telling me." She replaced the items in her backpack, slowly, one by one. When she'd finished, she left the backpack in the middle of the bed and stood next to the bed. Not getting too close to Rafe. His gentle brown eyes seemed out of place in such a big man.

"Let's go down to the living room and talk." Rafe left the room. She followed. It would be petty not to.

He'd settled onto the lumpy sofa, stretching out his long legs. She chose the lone chair in the small room. A stiff blue chair with a scratchy cover. She wouldn't sit near Rafe. She needed space between them.

"Tell me about your childhood in Oklahoma. How did you live? You said a grandmother raised you."

She squirmed in the uncomfortable chair, stalling. He'd listened earlier and now he wanted details. How much did she dare tell him? "My mother disappeared one morning when I was five. That left Granny and me." She raised her chin.

"Was that good or bad?"

"My mother was okay, but I didn't miss her. She was distant, didn't talk to me much. Maybe she was depressed, now that I think about it. My grandmother was upset when she left without me. She didn't want the responsibility of raising me."

"Where does the cousin fit into all this?"

A cold chill surged through her. "Nathan was my aunt's son. They lived next door. He was four years older. And mean. We weren't friends. He was my tormentor."

"What did he do to you?" His voice was as gentle as those big brown eyes.

She took a deep breath. She'd tell him part of it anyway. "He treated me like dirt. Like a bug you wanted to get rid of. Like a punching bag."

"He hit you?"

"Whenever he managed to be alone with me. I always had bruises."

"Couldn't your grandmother stop him?"

"She didn't care what he did. She always believed him and thought I was lying. Even when I showed her the bruises. She liked him."

"And she didn't like you?"

She turned away. "No. She slapped my face if I said something she didn't like."

"And Nathan used to hide things from you? Move your things around?"

"All the time. He wouldn't leave my toys and dolls alone."

He paused and just looked at her.

"Why did your grandmother kick you out of the house when you were fifteen?" A no nonsense tone of voice. He wanted answers.

"I was pregnant." She blurted out the words. And glared at him. She'd known all along her secret would have to come out. That's how investigations worked. She'd seen enough movies and television to know that.

He took a deep breath and seemed to be processing that information. "Who was the father?"

"Just a guy I knew who took advantage of me. He was older

than I was. And big and strong. He raped me." Her glare intensified.

"And nobody believed you."

She nodded.

"And that's why you're afraid of me?" He looked straight into her eyes and his gentle brown eyes said trust me. "That's why you're always afraid?" He leaned toward her. "I'll never take advantage of you. I'll never hurt you."

She relaxed the glare. "I know." She'd known him less than a day, yet she sensed the goodness in him.

"And the baby?" A gentle tone.

"Adopted out." She clamped her lips shut on *not by choice.* She swallowed those words just as she'd swallowed the pain of losing her baby. He didn't need to know everything, all her wounds. All her heartache.

"You were fifteen. Where did you go when you left home?"

"A social worker took me to a house in Kansas for pregnant teenage girls."

"I'm sorry you had a rough childhood." Rafe stood. "Now I understand why you believe it may be Nathan behind all this. But we need to figure out why after all these years."

"That's what's so puzzling." She looked up at him.

"Promise me one thing." Rafe said the words forcefully.

She just stared at him.

"Promise me you won't leave tonight. Let's see if he comes back and we catch him on the cameras. We went to a lot of trouble and expense putting in that equipment."

Blackmail. But he was right. It wouldn't be fair if she left tonight. After letting them do all they'd done so far. And she was beginning to trust him. "Okay, one night."

"It's a deal."

He reached out like he was going to shake her hand. She pulled away and he gave a half smile that said he understood.

That small smile said so much. She wouldn't leave tonight. She'd promised.

RAFE SETTLED into his work car for a long night. He drove his plain, dull brown Toyota when on a case. The kind of vehicle no one noticed when parked on a street. Its lack of comfort was the only problem.

He'd make sure Sabrina was safe from Nathan and wouldn't try to run tonight, despite her promise. He wouldn't blame her if she tried. He knew the kinds of things that made a person run. He'd done it himself.

He took out his cell phone and tapped Doug's number. Doug answered right away.

"I'm watching the house all night. The locks haven't been changed yet, so she definitely needs protection. Plus, she might run."

"You're going to stop her?" Doug's normally deep voice spiked at the end.

Rafe shifted in the uncomfortable seat. "Don't you want me to?" He ducked low enough to see the light escaping through a crack at the bottom of her bedroom curtains. He wanted her to stay, lead a normal life, be free.

"What makes you think she might leave? And why would she want to now?"

"She was checking the contents of her backpack when I got here earlier. It's ready for a quick get-away. I'd bet she's done it before."

"Run, you mean?"

"Yes. She's on edge right now and doesn't want to face that cousin of hers. She hasn't told me everything he's done."

"Why do you think that?" A demanding tone.

"Moving things around and hitting her when they were kids doesn't cause the kind of fear I'm seeing in her eyes. She's afraid of Nathan. I want to know why."

"Then keep asking questions. Force all you can out of her. We need facts and names." Doug was the pragmatic one.

"I did find out she was pregnant when she was kicked out at fifteen. And the baby was adopted out. I'm thinking maybe stolen from her, though she didn't admit that."

"I had a feeling there was more to her story." Doug's anger came through in his voice.

"She was defiant. Not happy I was questioning her. She'd like to keep secrets." Rafe leaned back in the seat. "She has that scared rabbit look in her eyes. I'm sure Nathan had done more than she's admitted."

"Okay, you've convinced me. I'll call Scott and see if he can relieve you at midnight, so you can get some sleep. I'll text you when I find out. You may have a full day tomorrow."

"Thanks. I was hoping we could make this a team effort. This case is more complicated than I originally thought."

"We're always a team. I have some ideas. Come in when you can leave her alone tomorrow morning."

"Will do."

"If this guy has come all the way from Oklahoma, I predict something else will happen real soon. Maybe tonight."

"Is that a hunch?"

"Based on a lot of years as a detective."

And Doug was a good detective. "This has to be more than harassment. When we figure out what he wants, we have him."

"Maybe."

"The reason lies in her past. In Oklahoma."

"If it's the cousin, it has to be Oklahoma. Keep prying those details out of her. Use your detective skills." Another ultimatum. Usual Doug talk.

Rafe slid down in his seat. "Someone came around the corner, from the direction of her shop. A man in a hooded sweatshirt."

"Let me know if it's anything." Doug ended the call.

Rafe stayed as low as he could and still see. The guy edged closer to the house, stood still for at least five minutes, then turned around and headed back the way he had come. The lights were still on inside the house. Rafe couldn't leave to follow the guy. He shifted his weight until he was situated where he could watch the corner and watch the house.

This case went far beyond simple surveillance and protection of property. Given Sabrina's degree of fear, her life could be at stake.

CHAPTER 5

Sabrina unlocked the front door of her shop and walked in, as if it were a normal day. It wasn't.

Rafe waited at the back door for her to let him in.

She wanted Nathan to go away. She wanted her normal life back. She wanted that big man to go away.

Taking a deep breath to settle her jumpy nerves, she hurried to the back door and opened it.

"Anything out of place?" Rafe was all business.

She glanced around. "No. I don't think so."

"Take a good look."

She took her time and looked at everything in the back room, then went to the front and checked out her displays. Rafe followed her. "Nothing. He usually makes it obvious."

She returned to the back room and set her backpack on her work table. "I wish I knew what he's going to do next."

"I'll look at the surveillance videos, to make sure he didn't come back."

"I want this over with." Her words came out in a wistful

tone.

"He must have a plan, a reason for breaking in here and letting you know it was him. That's what we have to figure out."

She sighed and glanced at her backpack. Rafe shook his head. "You can't go now. We have to see this through, see if he does come back, see what he does next time."

"I'm scared."

"I don't blame you. But we haven't caught him. He may follow you if you leave. He found you here."

"You're right." Her sigh came from deep down inside. "I don't know what he looks like now."

She sat in her chair behind the work table and straightened her long skirt.

"Something had to trigger his desire to find you. Erik is checking on those names you gave me."

"He might figure it out?"

"If we get lucky." Rafe crossed to the closet. "The surveillance videos will tell us if he came back and did something he didn't want you to see." He opened the closet with a key from his pocket. He took out a laptop and set it on the other side of her work table. Then he sat down, tapped a few keys, and stared at the monitor. "This shouldn't take long. The cameras are activated by motion detectors."

"I'll get to work. I have orders I need to get out." She unstacked her trays of gems and beads, opened her tool pouch, and glanced at the sales order on the top of her stack.

And tried to ignore Rafe. But he took up so much space in her little room. She concentrated on the one necklace, carefully stringing the gold beads and amber gemstones, tying them off, according to the pattern she'd done so many times before. Good thing it was a familiar pattern. She kept glancing at Rafe.

"Damn. Whoops, sorry about the language."

She raised her head. "You found something?"

He was staring at the screen, his face close. Then he got up and went to the small refrigerator that sat in the corner. He opened the door and just stared.

She stood, her heart beat accelerating. "What is it?" she demanded.

"I'm not sure. But he was in here and didn't want you to know." He backed up the images and then stopped the machine." Come around and watch this."

He pulled out a chair for her and she sat. Next to him. Too close. He pushed his chair back to give her room to view the screen. Someone in a hooded sweatshirt climbed through the window, leaving it open. Then this person went directly to the refrigerator. He took a small bottle out of his pocket and fumbled with something inside the refrigerator. Then put the bottle back in his pocket. Then closed the refrigerator door and climbed out the window, pulling it tight so it didn't look like it had been opened. Never showing his face.

A cold chill completely engulfed her body. "What did he do?"

"You saw what I saw. It looks like he put a liquid of some kind into something in the refrigerator. Don't eat or drink anything in there. I'm getting the police and their crime scene expert out here immediately." He pulled his cell phone from his pocket and punched in the number. "Nick, we have a case for you now. I think our suspect put poison in something in the refrigerator during the night. Send a team out right away." He ended the call.

Her shoulders started shaking. That cold chill intensified. "Poison?"

"It's possible. We have to have it checked out, to be sure."

"How soon will we know?"

"It may take several days to get the results back. Everything in there will have to be tested. We can't tell what he was doing because of the angle of the camera."

"Let me look at the picture of him again." She leaned forward. Rafe backed up the video until he had a good shot of the intruder, then paused the video.

"I haven't seen Nathan in fifteen years. His face is hidden. I have no way of knowing if it's him."

"I was afraid of that."

"What do we do now?"

"We'll have to get out of here while the investigation is going on. He's wearing thin plastic gloves so no fingerprints. I'll call Doug and tell him what happened and we can go to his office. The police will review the surveillance video and take everything from the refrigerator to get it tested."

Sabrina shivered. She was chilled so deeply she wasn't sure she'd ever be warm again.

Nathan could be trying to poison her.

THE BRICK-FACED AGENCY building wasn't as intimidating this time. But Sabrina's entire body tensed, like she was bound with a tight rope. Yet she was getting help.

I want my simple life back. A wail from her soul.

Rafe parked in the lot to the left of the building and they entered through the side door. Doug's office was in the back corner, with a window onto the side street. Not a fancy office but neat.

Doug was seated behind his desk and didn't get up when they came in. Like the last time she was here. Then she remembered that he'd used a cane when he was at her shop yesterday morning. Maybe an injury.

"Come on in." He smiled and gestured toward the chair. "Sit down."

"Thank you." She sat in the armed chair that Rafe pulled out for her, sinking onto the soft leather. Then she set her backpack on the floor by her feet. Doug glanced at the backpack, but didn't say anything. Rafe must have told him what was in her backpack.

"Why would your cousin want you dead?" No small talk. Doug got right down to business.

Such a direct question set her back for a moment. But he was a detective. She had to remember that. "I don't know for sure that he does." Though in her own heart she'd always known it was a possibility. "When I was ten, he told me he was going to kill me someday. But I thought he was just trying to scare me."

"And he was how old?" A frown creased Doug's forehead.

"Fourteen."

"Old enough to know better."

"This all started out as a nuisance. Now deadly? I'm not sure I believe it." She squirmed in the chair. "There's no reason, not after all this time."

"That's what we need to talk about." Doug's words were decisive. "Where have you lived besides Portland and Riley, Oklahoma?"

"Start at the beginning." Rafe's tone was gentle, like he was trying to put her at ease. The way he had at her shop and her house when he questioned her. "When you left Riley, you went to a home for unwed mothers. Where was it located?"

"Outside of the small town of Nielsen, Kansas. I'm sure most of the people around there had no idea who lived in that isolated farmhouse."

"Did the place have a name?"

"Not that I'm aware of. It was just a house with room for about six pregnant girls. They treated us real nice, until the baby was born."

"Then what happened?" Doug leaned forward, compassion on his face.

The words threatened to stick in her throat. "They took my baby, my tiny baby girl, and sold her on the adoption black market." She looked down at the floor. She couldn't look at the two men listening to her. They wanted details. Might as well get it over with. They would keep asking until she did.

She cleared her throat and raised her gaze to desk level. "The night I got to the house, it was late. I was very tired, because I'd tried to stay awake to see where the house was. Soon after I got there, the two women who ran the place had me sit at the dining room table. They had papers for me to sign. They were rushing me, not giving me time to read what I was signing. I was only fifteen. I guess I trusted them. I signed about five pieces of paper. Then they let me go upstairs and go to sleep."

"Did they tell you what you had signed?" Doug asked the question, his voice gentle.

Her stomach knotted. It took a lot of effort to get the words out. "Only after my baby girl was born and they had taken her away. I had my baby for three days. Then a nurse came in and asked to take the baby to examine her. Then someone gave me a shot that knocked me out. When I woke up my baby was gone."

She stopped and wiped at her eyes. "They let me stay three more days, then two big men took me to a bus station and put me on a bus to Seattle. They gave me twenty dollars, which was barely enough to buy food and water on the trip."

She looked up. Doug and Rafe were staring at her. Doug's eyes were moist.

"If that place is still in business, they soon won't be." Doug's words were emphatic and angry.

Some of the tension eased from her body. The truth was out. She hadn't realized how many lies she'd been living.

"Seattle." Rafe broke the silence. "What did you do when you got off that bus?"

"A man grabbed my arm as I stepped off the last step. He tried to steer me away from the terminal."

"How did you get away?"

"I was fighting him. A bag lady came to my rescue and beat him off with an umbrella."

Rafe smiled. "Then what?"

"Vivian, that was her name, took me in. I stayed in her camp all summer and she taught me how to make jewelry and sell it on the street."

"And you avoided the pimps?" Doug's voice held only compassion.

"Yes, with Vivian's help. It wasn't easy at times."

"How long have you been in Portland, and off the streets?" Doug's questions were probing, but gently phrased.

"About ten years. I'm thirty, in case you're curious. I know I don't look that old." She laughed at herself, self-consciously. At thirty, she was definitely the youngest in the room.

"And your business is supporting you now?" Another probing question from Doug.

"I make enough for food and rent and utilities, and a few other necessities. I live simply."

"You live in a house. Utility bills give people away all the time. Nathan may not have wanted to find you until now. The reason why is what we need to know." Doug stood. "I'll get Erik and see if he has anything yet on those names." He limped from the room.

Sabrina stared after him.

"A car bomb. It killed his wife and crippled him. Ended his police career." Rafe's words were quiet, reverent.

He started to reach out his hand, then pulled it back. He remembered she didn't want to be touched. Then he smiled gently at her. She was discovering what a nice man he was.

Doug returned with another man, much younger than he was, with dark blond hair and hazel eyes. He introduced him as Erik Bergstrom, the computer whiz at their agency.

Erik sat in the remaining chair, to the left of Doug's desk and Doug returned to his own chair. "Okay, Erik, what have you found so far?"

"Nathan left town on vacation a week ago. Said he was going on a cruise and would be gone at least two weeks. A sudden decision, I'm told. No advance planning that anyone was aware of. I've talked to the owner and two of his co-workers at the feed store where he works as a clerk."

What happened to his big plans? He always bragged about how successful he was going to be. He'd buy a fancy car. A nice boat for fishing on the lake. And a nice house.

"So he could be here. He probably drove." Disgust rode Rafe's tone. "A convenient vacation out of the country."

"I checked the airlines flying out of Oklahoma City and Dallas, to see if he booked a flight. He didn't."

"Good. Check every angle." Doug's emphatic voice.

"I've put in a request for his driver's license photo and the license plate number of the car he drives. I'll also get the make and model of the car."

"That will help." Doug's tone softened a bit. Not as commanding.

"Nathan's mother died several years ago of cancer." Erik looked straight at her. "Your mother died in an car accident in

Nevada over twenty years ago. I'm sorry, Sabrina." And his words echoed his sentiment. She was touched by his compassion. All the people she'd met in the agency were super nice to her.

Her mother. Dead. The news dropped on her like a damp Oregon drizzle. Barely noticeable. "She left when I was five. I hardly knew her."

She'd never known a mother's love. And she'd so wanted to be a good mother to her tiny baby. She blinked back tears that threatened.

"I did find your grandmother. She's in a nursing home in Riley. She's been there for five years. As a relative, you'll be able to get information on her condition."

If I want to know. The idea came unbidden. Did she hate her grandmother? No. She'd given her a home, at least. Until she kicked her out. "Thanks for finding all of this information." She managed a mumble.

"Good job, Erik." Doug nodded his head in Erik's direction. "Not much we can do until we get the results of the toxicology tests on the items in the refrigerator."

"Too bad one of the women couldn't stay with Sabrina in the shop during the day." Rafe said the words wistfully. Like he didn't want to be with her all day. And she certainly didn't want him there.

"So you can get some sleep. I hear you. Alison's trial ended in a plea bargain. She'll be free from tomorrow on. I'll arrange it." Doug looked at her. "Is that all right with you, Sabrina? Would you mind a little company until we know what's going on?"

"I'll be out on the street part of the day," Rafe said. "Scott agreed to split the night shift with me."

"This is getting complicated." Sabrina's tension returned. She shifted in her chair. "But it's okay. I don't mind the company." She couldn't leave now, not without hurting all these kind people. Unless Nathan got too close. Her fear of being alone and unprotected against Nathan warred with her need for solitude to do her creative work.

Doug smiled at her. "Okay. Alison Steele will accompany you to work, stay with you, and walk you back home every day."

"Are you okay with going back to work at the shop today?" Rafe directed his question at her.

"Do I dare?"

"As long as you don't eat or drink anything you don't take with you from home." Doug shifted in his chair so he was looking straight at her again. "We need to keep you on a normal schedule for now, so we don't spook him. When we find out what he put in the refrigerator, we'll know what kind of response is needed to catch him."

"That makes sense. I'll open the shop and work on my jewelry." And hope nothing more happens today. She shuddered and reached for her backpack.

"I won't be far away."

She glanced at Rafe and saw something in those gentle brown eyes that she wasn't sure how to interpret. Something she wasn't used to seeing in a man's eyes.

Her simple life was getting more complicated with each passing hour. Someone with her day and night. No more privacy. The soulful wail inside became louder.

CHAPTER 6

*R*afe hesitated outside the back door to Sabrina's shop. Lunchtime. And Sabrina didn't have food in her refrigerator to eat.

He'd brought her directly here after they left Doug's office. Taking her out to lunch would be the polite thing to do.

The problem was his growing interest in her. He looked forward to seeing her again. He had to keep thinking of her solely as someone needing help, as a client of the agency. Doug had warned him. Yet he wasn't heeding his own internal warning.

He knocked on the back door.

The door opened slowly and she peeked out. Obviously not expecting him to return.

His heart rate did a little skip. "Hi. I was getting ready to go grab a hamburger for lunch and I know you don't have anything here to eat."

"I was going to lock up and go home for lunch."

"Lock up and come with me, if you'd like a hamburger. Or do you eat hamburgers?"

"I'm not a vegetarian, if that's what you're wondering." She stared at him, her brows furrowed, her eyes in a half-squint. Like she was suspicious of his motives. "You don't have to take me with you. I can get my own lunch."

She backed up. Was she still afraid of him? He didn't blame her, after all she'd been through. What she'd revealed in Doug's office this morning raised his opinion of her abilities and her spirit quite a few notches.

"I know I don't have to take you, but I want to." He tried for a disarming smile. "We can't have one of our clients going hungry. Let's go eat."

She still hung back.

"A nice juicy hamburger with all the trimmings?" He was determined to get her to agree, though he was stepping over a line.

Her lips quivered, like she was trying to suppress a smile. "You do know how to persuade." She shoved her computer and her cell phone into her backpack, zipped it, and slung it over her shoulder. He was going to protest they weren't going far, but he didn't.

Her security blanket. He got that.

"I'm going with you because you're my bodyguard." A challenging tone.

"Yes, I'm your bodyguard. I'll keep you safe." Even from himself.

FLUTTERS in her stomach kept Sabrina on edge as she walked

down the street at Rafe's side. She wasn't a tiny woman. But he was definitely a big man. He had to be over six feet tall.

They'd gone three blocks when Rafe stopped and opened the door of a small cafe. "You picked a good place. I've eaten here." Quiet words. She regretted saying yes. She wasn't the least bit comfortable with this man.

"Doug brought me here the first time. He loves hamburgers too. Even though it's not close to the office, we come here occasionally."

Rafe's hand touched her upper back, guiding her through the door. Alarm bells went off in her mind and body. Her heart rate sped up. She surged forward, breaking the contact with his hand, straight to a booth by the front window.

A waitress followed and set down menus. "I'll be right back to take your orders." She scurried away.

Rafe sat across from her. "I'm sorry. I shouldn't have touched you." He picked up his menu but kept his gentle eyes on her.

She turned away from his probing gaze. She wasn't about to tell him how men had tried to take advantage of her over the years, when she was destitute and alone. He knew she'd lived on the streets for a while. He could figure it out.

She glanced at the menu, decided on that juicy hamburger. And fries. And water to drink.

The waitress returned and took her order first.

Rafe ordered the hamburger and fries, then added a straw-berry shake. He looked at her. "Wouldn't you like a shake too?"

She hesitated. Could she? His crooked smile dared her to say yes. She answered with her own half smile, then looked up at the waitress. "I'd like a chocolate shake."

His smile widened. He was a nice man. Not a taker, but a giver. She relaxed a little.

Could she use this time with Rafe to ask some questions?

Find out what she wanted to know about the agency? About Doug? About him?

She was trusting people she didn't know. They were taking over her life. To keep her safe. She got that. But it bothered her. Her privacy was gone.

Rafe was intelligent. She'd seen how systematic and thorough he'd been setting up the surveillance at her shop and finding the problems at her house. And acting professional the entire time.

She hesitated, those flutters in her stomach doing flip flops. She blurted out, "Are you just a bodyguard or a detective looking for clues? Or...or...or...?"

"I thought you were going to explode, you were looking so nervous. I'm an ex-cop who's now a detective and a bodyguard and a handyman, or whatever is required on the jobs that come to Doug's agency. Are you concerned that I might not be able to protect you?"

She was concerned about that electric smile of his. "No... no... I saw what you did yesterday and this morning. You know what you're doing."

"But you're still not convinced I can keep you safe?"

She closed her eyes, gathering her thoughts. How could she explain this? She opened her eyes and looked into the gentle brown depths of his. And a prick of panic hit her. She liked him. A lot. He was kind and gentle and good, from what she'd seen so far.

"I'm not concerned about you, or...Doug. How long ago was he injured?" The words came out fast.

"Five years. Down in L.A., and the drug lord he was after tried to kill him. His legs were shattered and had to be put back together with steel rods."

"Oh, my. How awful for him." Total respect shone in Rafe's eyes. His boss was a good man too. She was sure of that.

Rafe leaned back in the booth and stretched out his legs. "And now that drug lord is back from Mexico, where he fled. He's threatening to move his operations up here, and come after Doug too."

"Why?"

"Doug shot and killed Moreno's two sons during a drug raid. That's why the car bomb. That's why he'll try again to kill Doug."

The waitress delivered their shakes. Sabrina put her straw into the glass, and took a drink, letting the cold chocolate goodness slide down her throat. "Will Doug be able to take care of himself when the guy comes after him?"

"We'll all help Doug take down Moreno. He's made millions off illegal drugs sold on the streets of Los Angeles and other cities. Now he plans to expand to Portland and Seattle, and get rid of Doug too."

"Oh, dear. So Doug waits and wonders when this guy will strike. I hope Doug doesn't get killed. He's a nice man."

"Yeah. He is."

The waitress delivered their hamburgers and fries. That first bite of hamburger tasted so good. She couldn't remember the last time she'd splurged on a restaurant meal. It had been a long time. And a shake? Years.

She finished half the hamburger and half the fries before she was ready with more questions.

"Poison? I can hardly believe someone would deliberately try to poison me. If it was Nathan, why now? I can't come up with any answers."

Rafe frowned and set down his almost finished hamburger. "We always want instant answers. Investigations aren't like that.

We sift through what we have and come up with possible motives."

He finished off his hamburger and wiped his mouth with his napkin. Then tackled the shake. He was thinking. She could tell by that frown and the piercing look in his eyes. Those dark eyes that saw so much.

"Why would he want you dead?" He stared at her. Stirring up those flutters in her stomach again. "Are you sure you didn't do something that he's holding against you? A grudge for some reason? Think real hard."

She bristled at Rafe's tone. He sounded like he blamed her. "No way. He picked on me all the time. I didn't have a chance to get back at him."

"You don't remember anything you did? Anything at all?" Rafe looked closely at her, as if studying her reaction.

"He made sure I got blamed for stuff. His favorite phrase was, 'I seen her do it, Granny.' He always had that big innocent, wide-eyed look. He was a total fraud. Had Granny completely fooled."

"Okay, I'm getting the picture." A grimace accompanied his words. "But there has to be a reason. He's gone to a lot of trouble. He took a sudden vacation."

"Maybe it's a game to him. Maybe he was bored with life." She shrugged.

"No, it has to be more than that. He's playing for keeps."

"You don't know if it was poison in the refrigerator. You don't know if it's Nathan. And I couldn't tell from that video."

"We only know that whoever it was poured something into something in that refrigerator." He emphasized his words.

She leaned against the back of the seat, her chocolate shake in her hand. "So we wait for the results of the tests."

"Yes. And we go on taking precautions until we find him or figure out his motive. I'm not letting him get you, Sabrina."

"You can't guard me every minute." Disbelief laced her words.

"Almost. We're arranging schedules so you won't be alone until he's captured. And we know what's going on."

"Doug said Alison would be in the shop with me. Since Nathan or whoever didn't do anything during the day, I don't think that's necessary." The words came out sharper than she'd intended.

"Doug does. And so do I."

"Surely Nathan won't try something in the middle of the day."

"We don't know that. Alison Steele is a crack shot. The best shot in the agency. Better than Doug."

"I still don't think it's necessary."

"I do. I'll be in your house or outside of it at night. We'll all be watching. When I'm inside the house getting some sleep on the couch, Scott Armstrong will be outside on the street. He's another very capable agency member. Been with Doug since the beginning. A very good man to have on your team."

"Will I meet him?"

"I'll bring him by the shop later and introduce you."

"Okay." Rafe downstairs while she slept? Another huge complication. Those flutters got stronger.

If she wanted to stay in Portland, she'd have to take her chances with Rafe. And hope she hadn't misjudged him.

CHAPTER 7

Holy shit! Rafe sat up straight on the wooden chair. Sabrina had padded into the kitchen on bare feet. The dim glow from the night light was enough that he could tell she wore a long light-colored T-shirt. And no bra. The shirt hung down far enough to cover any panties she might have been wearing.

Rafe's mouth went dry. He couldn't have moved if he'd wanted to.

She filled a glass with water from the tap. Then turned sharply and looked right at him, and almost dropped the glass. "Oh, I didn't know you were in here."

"Are you all right? Did something wake you?"

"I need a drink." She gulped down the water, then dropped the glass on the counter. Edging away from him, she ran from the kitchen and up the stairs, her footsteps pounding on the bare wood.

Damn! Now he knew what kind of body was beneath all those clothes. With her running around the house like that, he'd have a permanent arousal. Keeping his personal feelings out of this assignment was getting more difficult by the day. He genuinely liked Sabrina. She was a mystery he wanted to solve. A woman in need. Double damn. Doug had warned him off.

He checked his watch. Time to relieve Scott so he could go home. The rest of the night shift was his responsibility. He'd slept four hours on the couch before coming into the kitchen.

Rafe went to his car, parked three houses down the street, and got behind the wheel. Scott saw him come out and started his own car and pulled away. He drove to the far end of the street before turning on his lights and disappearing around the corner.

A smooth transition. They'd done this kind of hand off many times doing street surveillance. Sometimes it paid off. Rafe scooted down in the seat so he could see out the window but wasn't visible from a distance.

Thirty minutes later, a man in a hooded sweatshirt walked down the deserted street, from the direction of the shop. He stopped across from Sabrina's house and stood there for a minute. Then he turned and went back the way he'd come. Probably the same man Rafe had seen the night before.

So he was watching the house too. The police would have to catch the guy. Nick said there'd be regular patrols by the shop.

His role was to stay here. Sabrina's life could be at stake. When this was over, he'd go on to another assignment and try to get sweet Sabrina out of his mind. Maybe the most difficult part of this whole job.

SABRINA LOCKED the front door of the shop and joined Alison at the end of the alley. Alison had come out the back door and was waiting for her. She didn't look like a detective, like the crack shot Rafe said she was. She had the look of an office worker. Chin-length blond hair that curved around her face, a wide smile, and soft blue eyes. But under her light jacket she wore a holster and gun.

Three days of the same routine. She and Alison walked the short distance from the shop to the house, both alert and watching for anyone lurking. They reached the front door. Alison knocked and Rafe opened the door. Sabrina went inside, waving a goodbye to Alison.

"Roast chicken tonight?" Rafe's electric smile made her heart beat faster. "It's almost ready."

A delicious aroma came from the kitchen. She panicked. "You don't have to cook for me every night." She tried to keep the exasperation out of her tone, but couldn't. It crept through.

"I have to eat too. Besides, I like to cook. It's a way to relax." He retreated to the kitchen door.

She set her backpack on the couch and followed him into the kitchen. "Are you buying all this food?"

"I've done the shopping. Doug's paying. And don't say he doesn't have to. He wants to, or he wouldn't be doing it." He gave her a sharp look.

"Okay." Nobody had ever taken care of her like this before. What she missed was the life she'd built for herself. Her solitude. Her privacy.

"I never learned to cook. Granny didn't want me in the kitchen. I've always eaten what was easy to get. As long as it was filling."

"So canned soup and microwave dinners? That's all I found in here."

"And sandwiches. They're filling." This time her tone was defensive. He was criticizing her.

"I taught myself to cook. I'll give you some lessons if you want."

"I don't know. I'll go wash up." She headed up the stairs to her bedroom and put her backpack by the bed in its accustomed place. Then escaped to the bathroom to calm down. It was getting harder and harder to get through a day, with all these people around. They made her jittery and defensive. Rafe scared her still, but for a big man he was also gentle. Like he was afraid to hurt her. A welcome change from past experiences.

When she emerged from the bathroom, she heard voices downstairs in the kitchen. Male voices. She crept down the stairs, then hung back in the living room, not wanting to go into the kitchen. She thought she recognized Doug's voice, and maybe the other one was that Nick that Rafe called after he looked at the video.

"Sabrina." Rafe called her name. The man was uncanny. He must have heard her come down the stairs.

She went into the kitchen, though reluctant. Why were they at her house?"

Doug and the other man stood near the stove with Rafe.

Rafe gestured toward the other man. "This is Nick Castellani, the police detective who's in charge of the investigation now."

"Oh, Tricia's husband. I didn't know you were a detective." She felt a bit better. Another big man with kind dark eyes.

"We'll find this guy, Sabrina." Nick smiled at her.

Doug used his cane and limped to the table, sitting in one of the two chairs. "Sabrina, we have some bad news for you."

Nick pulled out the other chair for her and waited until she sat. "One of the water bottles in the front of the refrigerator contained a deadly poison."

Her heart rate spiraled upward, knocking at her chest wall. "Someone wants me dead?" Her voice shook and a deep chill settled in her bones. In all the years she'd been on the run, she'd never felt completely at risk. Now, living in a city with nice people, she faced her worst challenge. Someone wanted her dead.

Was it Nathan?

She shrunk back into herself, the scared little girl again. Sitting in the tree, waiting for her grandmother to come home. She couldn't go in the house when her grandmother wasn't there. That's when Nathan was at his worst. That's when he couldn't keep his hands to himself. Especially as she got older.

"If you had started to drink that water, you would have died." Doug's voice seemed to come out of the air. Suspended. Unreal. This couldn't be happening.

"Why?" Shock waves pulsed through her. "Why would someone do that to me?" She felt like shouting, but kept her voice low.

Rafe turned off the oven and the burner on the stove. "What was the poison used? Can we trace it?"

"Possibly. They found sodium fluoroacetate in the water." Nick's tone was not the least bit reassuring. "This stuff was used as a rat killer in barns years ago, but resulted in accidental poisonings until it was banned in the U.S. for general sales. It's only available by special license to kill coyotes."

Sabrina sat still, stunned into silence. A deadly poison that could have killed her.

Nick turned to her. "This is now my case, as lead detective. We're looking for any businesses near where Nathan lives that sell sodium fluoroacetate. He got it from somewhere."

"Maybe that feed store where he works." Doug's tone was grim.

"Why would he use that particular poison?" Rafe leaned against the window sill, opposite the table.

Nick moved over to the counter by the stove. "It's colorless, odorless, a small amount kills in a very short time. Some people last only minutes. Hardy souls last a few hours."

Rafe looked at Doug, then at Nick. "So, what do we do now? Is she safe enough with the routine we've established?"

"I think so." Doug used his emphatic voice. "I'll have Dave roam around both the house and the shop areas on his bike. I'll bring him by tomorrow and introduce him to Sabrina, so she knows he's one of us."

He smiled at her. "Dave Quinlan is usually on his motorcycle, but sometimes rides a high end bicycle. Whatever is needed for the type of surveillances he does for us. Right now he's working an insurance fraud case but can spare some time to help us keep you safe."

She nodded but didn't say anything.

"Have you ever heard anyone talk about sodium fluoroacetate?" Doug looked straight at her.

"No. I've never heard of it."

"Riley is a small town, with farms around it, isn't it?" Rafe pushed off from the window sill and moved closer to her.

"Yes, lots of small farms. The feed store stays busy."

"Start there, Nick." Doug's commanding tone. He even ordered the police around.

"We already have. I'm getting help within the precinct to search for the source of the sodium fluoroacetate. To find out who bought it and when. Or if there's any missing from some inventory. Not only in Riley, but surrounding towns."

She took a deep breath to calm herself. It was all so unreal, so unbelievable. Someone wanted her dead. Nathan wanted her dead. It could only be him. No one else hated her like he did.

Rafe gazed at her, his expression full of compassion. "Anything else you can tell us?"

"Nathan used to say, when we were kids, that he'd kill me someday to get rid of me." She squeaked out the words. Her throat constricted and kept her from projecting her voice.

Doug reached over and patted Sabrina's hand. "If it's Nathan, we'll find him. In the meantime, we'll make sure you're safe." Somehow the gesture from Doug was soothing, not scary.

"Are you checking motels in this area?" Rafe asked.

"That's my job. The legwork." Nick shrugged. "So far nothing has turned up."

Doug took a piece of paper from an inside pocket of his jacket and handed it to Nick. "Erik didn't find any criminal record for Nathan, so there aren't any mug shots. But he did get an emailed copy of his driver's license photo."

Nick took the paper and looked at it closely. "Not a clear picture. Is this what he's driving, down here on the bottom of the page? And the license plate number?"

"Yes. State records listed a 1982 Ford Fairlane registered to him."

"Maybe that's old Mr. Nickerson's car." The information surprised her. Nathan liked fancy cars. "A dirty brown thing he hardly ever drove as he got older."

The three men looked at her. "You'd recognize the car if you saw it?" Rafe's question.

"Yes."

"I'll find a better picture online and send out an alert. We have the plate number."

Nick set the page in front of her. The blurry picture of Nathan. She forced herself to look at it. The pointed chin. The stark blue eyes and bushy brows. He was nineteen the last time she saw him. He hadn't changed much.

"Does he look familiar?" Doug reached out and patted her hand again. "And if you see the car, call 911 immediately. We'll get him."

"He does look familiar." She murmured the words. A shudder passed through her.

Rafe leaned against the counter, next to Nick. "What if I took Sabrina to Oklahoma and we talked to people she knew as a child? Might get information on Nathan that way."

"You wouldn't be able to act as an investigator in another state." She recognized Doug's official voice again. "You'd be relegated to bodyguard and support team. Sabrina would have to ask the questions."

"That should work." Rafe turned to her. "Is there a town gossip?"

Her stomach knotted, a twisting ache of dread. Go back to Riley? Back to where she felt so small and insignificant?

The three men in her tiny kitchen waited. And watched her intently.

"Town gossip? At least a person who knows everyone in town. That would be Mrs. Murphy, who runs the grocery store."

"Erik can find out if she's still there." Doug looked up at Rafe. "I like that idea. It gets Sabrina out of town for a few days. But you'd have to be extremely careful."

"The patrol cars can keep a watch on the shop." Nick's expression turned to a full smile. "We might catch him while you're gone."

Sabrina gazed at Rafe, at the grim lines of his face. Could she go that far with him? Did she dare trust him that much? She'd have to dig deep down inside to find the courage if she made this trip. At least Nathan wasn't in Riley.

"Are you willing to go?" Doug's gentle question surprised her.

She could refuse. "I'd like to see Granny while she's still alive." The knot in her stomach grew harder. She'd surprised herself.

A part of her wanted to go. The little girl part.

CHAPTER 8

A totally nerve wracking day. And it wasn't over yet. Sabrina squirmed in the seat of the rental SUV and glanced at Rafe. He'd hunkered down over the steering wheel, his gaze intent on the two lane highway heading south. Riley couldn't be too much further.

Her stomach clenched tighter with each mile they traveled. She could have said no. Doug asked her. She wasn't ordered to come with Rafe.

Rafe.

At least she wasn't sitting as close to him in the car as she had been in that crowded plane. She'd never flown before and didn't realize she'd be sandwiched in between two big men. Rafe had immediately seen her discomfort and switched places with her, so she had the aisle seat. That helped a little.

But being that close to Rafe, shoulders touching at times, had sparked tingling sensations in her body she'd never ever felt. That scared her.

"Looking familiar yet?"

She glanced from side to side, still able to make out trees and houses, despite the approaching dusk.

"No. I've rarely been this far north on this road. Granny didn't drive. We never went to Oklahoma City."

"You're getting a real education today. You've never flown before."

"You could tell."

"I've been feeling guilty all day about putting you through this. I wasn't thinking about the effect on you."

Another reminder of his compassion. "That's okay. I said I would come."

"I don't know about you, but I'm ready for a good night's sleep."

That tightness in her stomach became a hard rock. Two rooms. She heard Doug say rooms. She held onto that thought.

"Not much to look at on this long drive. Oklahoma is relatively flat."

"Not like Oregon. But it has pecan trees. Big oaks. Lots of other trees. I guess I missed the pecan trees after I left here." She looked out the window. "There's one, in front of that house."

He glanced at the tree, then back at the road. "Why a pecan tree? Do you like pecan pie?"

"They were good for hiding in, until Nathan figured it out and started looking up for me."

"You had to hide from him?" Disbelief lodged in his tone.

"As much as I could."

"He was that mean?"

"He was that mean." She emphasized the words.

"We'll get him. If he's here and not in Portland, I'll scare the living daylights out of him."

And Rafe could. He'd scared her and he was being nice to her.

67

"We're getting close to Riley. I recognize that corner up ahead. Turn right there."

Rafe made the turn and followed the road for a little ways. When they rounded a bend, the short main street came into view.

"This is Riley. Those four blinking lights at those intersections weren't here before."

"Fifteen years. Some things will have changed." A matter-of-fact statement that was typical Rafe talk.

"That's all I see so far that's different. Just a small midwestern town that never grew up."

He looked at her funny.

"I meant that it doesn't change because the people are rigid and uncompromising."

"And I thought I was the cynical one."

He drove through the center of town and Sabrina looked for familiar stores and shops. She didn't expect to see anyone she'd known. Especially out at night. Undoubtedly many people had stayed. And she'd have to look for them and find out what she could. Find out the local gossip. That's why she was here. With Rafe.

Rafe said she'd play the role of investigative reporter and question people. She wasn't sure she could. She didn't like doing anything to bring attention to herself. That's how she'd survived growing up and how she'd survived on the streets of Seattle and Portland.

She'd go back to her isolated life as soon as Nathan was caught.

They stopped for a late dinner at a small restaurant and Sabrina didn't see anyone she knew. Then they headed to their motel, the only one in town. A typical small town motel. One level. A small office in the middle, separating the two sections.

Living quarters behind the office. Rooms on the front and the back of each section.

They'd go to the nursing home first thing in the morning. That lump in her stomach got harder. Facing Granny would be the most difficult part of this trip.

Rafe closed the door of the motel behind them and set down the two suitcases he'd brought in. Sabrina looked around the room and saw only one bed. Her heart sank.

Then Rafe unlocked a door in the wall and opened it. "You can have this adjoining room. I'll leave the connecting door unlocked, so I can come running if anything happens. Which I don't expect."

"No one knows we're back here except agency people and the police?"

"That's right. We simply locked up your shop. Maybe your customers will assume you're sick."

She slipped through the door he held open. Another room with one bed. She breathed a sigh of relief. He was being careful, getting two rooms that had a door in the middle. The room was clean. Nothing left over from previous tenants.

He picked up her suitcase and followed her into the room. "Is this okay? You don't look like you approve." He set the suitcase down at the end of the bed.

"I was just thinking that I've never been in a motel this nice."

He looked at her quizzically.

"When I was on the streets, when I had the money, I'd occasionally rent a motel room for one night so I could shower and wash my hair and sleep in a clean bed. A real treat."

"Yeah, I remember those days. I haven't told you, but I lived on the streets for one summer before I found a job and could afford to rent a room."

"Oh. I never thought about you living anywhere but a nice place."

"Don't look so shocked." He sat in the lone chair in the room. That lump in her stomach came back. He wasn't leaving her alone yet.

She set her backpack next to her suitcase and sat on the edge of the bed. "I guess I'm making assumptions. Because I don't know you very well."

"I haven't told you much about my life. I guess I should. Then you'll understand why I'm so determined to help you so you don't have to run again."

"You've run too?"

"The first time when I was fifteen. I was living in a small town in upstate New York, not much different than Riley. You said you'd never known your father. I wish I'd never known mine." He hesitated. Maybe wondering how much to tell her.

Rafe looked right at her, simmering anger flashing in his eyes. "He was an abusive SOB with hair-trigger rage. When I came into the house that day, I heard shouting, two shots, and a blood-curdling scream. I opened the door into the bedroom and my father was standing over my mother and my twelve-year-old sister. They were on the floor. Blood all over. The gun still in his hand. I slammed the door and ran like hell, right out the front door and across the field, heading for the woods. My father fired two shots after me, but missed. Then I heard more shots from the house. I never went back."

Horror washed through her. "That's terrible. He killed your mother and sister."

"Terrible things happen to people. I called a friend several weeks later and he told me my mother had five bullets in her, my sister had three. Neither had a chance to survive. The deputy sheriff shot and killed my father when they found him the next day and he fired at them."

"I've been so wrapped up in my own misery, I've never given a thought to what other people might have in their own pasts. I should know better. A lot of people live on the streets."

"You were trying to survive. Just as I was. The second time I ran was when I was a cop and I shot the man who killed my wife. And my unborn daughter."

Her heart clenched like it had been hit with a dart. His wife. His daughter. He lost a daughter. "Why are you telling me all this?"

"Because I want you to know where I'm coming from. Why I do what I do. And why you need to listen to me when it comes to your safety. I've been there. Believe me."

"Oh, I do believe you. Do you think there's a chance the police can catch Nathan and I can stop running?"

"Yes. You have a very powerful team of people on your side. In case you hadn't noticed, Doug has everyone in the agency helping in some way. Except Kara. But she'll join in when she gets back. That's how we get things done."

She looked down at the floor. "I'm scared of what Nathan will try next. He's a bad person. He was a bully and mean and vicious when he was young. I doubt he's changed."

Rafe stood. "You have. You've learned how to take care of yourself. You have a business and a home."

She shifted her position on the bed, scooting back a bit. "I still feel like a fraud at times. Like I don't belong."

"We all have such moments. And now we need to get some sleep. We'll start with the nursing home tomorrow. And see your grandmother. Once we know how she's been taken care of, we'll decide what to do next."

"I have to go there. But I'm afraid to face her."

Rafe moved close to the door. "She may not know you anymore. Often people in nursing homes have dementia and forget even their closest relatives. And she hasn't seen you in years."

"I'd like to talk to her and tell her my side of the story."

"You may not get that chance."

Her spirits plummeted further. "I hope she knows me, I hope I can stand up for myself with her. I'm not sure I'm that strong."

"Believe in yourself, Sabrina." With that, he walked through the door and closed it behind him.

She stared at the door. She shouldn't have come back here. What she'd face tomorrow scared her.

SABRINA STIFLED a yawn as she got out of the SUV the next morning. She hadn't been able to sleep until she'd heard Rafe's heavy snores from the next room.

She looked up at the old red brick building. The nursing home hadn't changed. Still surrounded by huge elms. The new greens of spring sprouted on the bushes and trees. The building itself was cold looking and depressing.

Rafe pulled the front door open and held it for her. She breathed in the odor of a peculiar mix of chemicals and aging building. And shivered.

The woman at the front desk gave them Granny's room number and general directions. Her tone was bored, the directions curt.

They entered a room with four beds, and four sleeping women. Sabrina glanced around, her panic growing. "I don't know which one is Granny."

Rafe stepped out into the hall, stopped an aide, and asked for Lila Faye Walters.

The aide poked her head into the room. "First bed by the door." She slipped away before Sabrina could ask any questions.

The shriveled old woman lying in the first bed didn't look like the Granny she remembered. Sabrina's heart did a strange flip flop, tightening and racing simultaneously. Granny had been a robust woman, always slightly overweight. With a commanding look about her. No one crossed her without consequences.

Now she was a shell of a person, curled up on her side, eyes closed, breathing shallow. Sabrina moved closer, her heart still racing. She reached down and stroked her arm. "Granny, I'm here. It's Sabrina." Granny didn't move or acknowledge her in any way. Sabrina choked back tears. "It's so sad seeing her this way. I really wanted to talk to her."

Rafe moved to her side. "Erik said she'd been here five years. People usually don't live too long in nursing homes. They deteriorate rather quickly. Especially if they don't have family around to visit with them and see to their care."

"And Nathan wouldn't do anything to make things easier for her." She patted the frail hand covered with broken blood vessels. An IV line had been inserted in her arm. "I'll have to call her doctor and find out what's being done for her."

She glanced at the light blanket that covered her. And the stains on the blanket. She lifted it. And her heart raced into overdrive. Oozing sores on Granny's buttocks were visible where her gown had pulled away. "Oh my, look at these bed sores. And look how dirty the sheets and blanket are. They aren't being changed every day."

Rafe leaned over, took a quick look, then moved away. "You're right. She's not getting good care here."

Sabrina replaced the soiled blanket. "We won't get any information from Granny. She doesn't look like she'll live much longer. Probably a good thing. What a horrible place to have to live. And die."

"No one deserves this kind of treatment," Rafe said. "Let's shake things up a bit. We'll let people know we're here and mean business."

"What can we do?" She took a deep breath, willing her heart to slow down so she could think straight.

"Have them get her cleaned up for starters."

Rafe went into the hallway and stopped another aide passing by. "We need someone in here to tend to Mrs. Walters."

"I can't help you. I got work to do."

Rafe poked his head around the door frame. "I'll get some action." He headed down the hallway toward the front door.

If anyone could get something done, it was Rafe. He always seemed to know what to do. In a few minutes he returned with a man dressed in slacks and a white shirt, looking very official.

"This is the manager of the facility, Sabrina. Donald Tennel."

She turned to the man, her anger rising. "My grandmother is in a filthy bed and has bed sores. I want this bed changed and my grandmother bathed and her sores treated. I'll be reporting this home to the authorities if something isn't done immediately." Her words gushed out in a torrent.

The manager lifted the soiled blanket and his brows rose. "I'll take care of it."

He left the room and came back two minutes later with two aides, one carrying clean linens and a clean gown for her grandmother. The other carried a pan for water for bathing her.

"Let's go." Rafe motioned to her. "And let them do their work."

She patted her grandmother on the arm. "I'm leaving, Granny. But I'll be back."

"Whoever is taking care of her affairs is going to hear about this. Her care here is inexcusable." Anger rode the edge of Rafe's voice.

The manager left hurriedly.

"I'll call her doctor and ask him why he's not taking better care of her." Sabrina moved toward the door.

She stood in the hallway for a minute. Looking back at Granny being tended to. The aides hadn't closed the door to protect her modesty.

Granny was probably beyond help. Sabrina's heavy heart filled her chest. She was glad she'd come. Even though Granny hadn't treated her right when she was a child, Sabrina couldn't let her die in a filthy bed. This nursing home was guilty of elder abuse. Maybe her doctor too. A call to him was next on her list.

CHAPTER 9

*R*afe opened the door of the SUV and Sabrina got in, her heart heavy with grief. "How can people sleep at night when they treat another human being that poorly?"

Rafe didn't start the engine. "I'm sorry you didn't get to talk to her. I'm sorry she's being neglected. I'm sorry you're hurting."

She gazed at him. At those soft brown eyes full of compassion.

"I'm also very proud of the way you stood up for your grandmother. I don't think they'll neglect her anymore."

"I'll be leaving Riley. I won't be here to check on her."

"Is there anyone in town who might be willing to look in on your grandmother occasionally, to make sure she's not left in filth again?"

"Maybe one of her old friends. One of the women she used to play cards with in the afternoon. When she left me to face Nathan alone after school."

"I'm not liking your grandmother very much."

She laughed. A quick bitter laugh. "I didn't like her very

much when I was growing up. But I feel sorry for her now. And I won't stand for her being mistreated."

"Good." He started the SUV and headed for the motel. "You realize don't you that we're going to make some enemies while we're here in town?"

"I don't care. I don't live here. I want information and I want Granny treated properly. Then I can go back to Portland with a clear conscience."

"Are you ready to make some telephone calls?"

A slight panic rose inside her. "What if they won't talk to me?"

"Then we'll know they have something to hide and we'll investigate them further. Doug can hire an Oklahoma PI to ask the questions I can't, because of my Oregon PI license."

"I want to know why Nathan wants me dead."

"We're just assuming it's him."

"My gut feeling tells me it's him. That gum wrapper. Moving things around. And the vacation he's supposedly taking? A cruise? That's so not like him."

"We may not find all the answers on this trip. But we'll work as many angles as possible."

He pulled into the motel parking lot and stopped in front of the door to his room. "Let's go make those calls."

Sabrina followed Rafe into the motel room and took out her cell phone and the list Erik had given her. Using the telephone number Erik had found for her, she dialed the number of the doctor's office where her grandmother had been treated for years. Then she sat in the chair by the small desk. Her hand shook as she held the phone. She hated confrontation and she knew what was coming. She felt as small and insignificant as she had as a child growing up in Riley.

Rafe sat on the bed, a smug smile lit his face. "This ought to be interesting."

"I need to talk to Dr. Atkins, please. I'm Sabrina Walters, the granddaughter of Lila Faye Walters. I'm concerned about her condition and how she's being treated at the nursing home."

"He's not available for phone consultations," the receptionist said. "You'll have to make an appointment and come in to see him."

"Okay, give me an appointment for today or tomorrow, please."

"That's impossible. You'll have to wait until late next week."

"That's ridiculous. My grandmother is being mistreated in that nursing home. If I can't talk to the doctor today, I'll go to the police station and report elder abuse. I want action now."

"Bravo. Go get them, tiger." Rafe's words encouraged her.

Silence on the line. She waited.

"This is Dr. Atkins. What seems to be the problem? Why are you making threats?"

"Because of the rudeness of your receptionist. And I'm upset. I was at the nursing home to see my grandmother and she has bed sores and was lying in a bed with dirty sheets and blanket. As her attending physician, why haven't you seen to her comfort? The poor woman is dying and is being treated like an animal." Once she started talking the words tumbled out like rocks down a mountain.

"I have no control over conditions at the nursing home."

"Then why hasn't she been moved to a better facility?"

"That costs money. I'm not in charge of her finances, just her medical care." The exasperation was evident in his voice.

"Who pays her bills?" Sabrina's annoyance grew at the super-cilious tone he was using with her, like she was a child who was being naughty.

"Her account is in Hornsby's bank. Her lawyer signs the checks. You'll have to talk to them about her finances. I can't tell you anything. You're wasting my time. Your grandmother is getting good care."

"No she isn't. I saw the bed and how filthy it was. And the bed sores. Why haven't you treated her for those bed sores?"

"I wasn't informed of any such sores."

"And you don't regularly check her over? What kind of doctor are you?" Her voice escalated in tone.

"What kind of granddaughter are you? You finally came back, as the old lady is dying. To get your inheritance, I suppose." The words were cutting and struck a chord deep inside of Sabrina. Yes, she was feeling guilty that she hadn't checked on the welfare of her grandmother, since leaving Riley. Her only excuse her anger at being tossed out at fifteen and losing her baby to those thieves.

"I came back because I found out she was in a nursing home. I wanted to see her, even though she probably wouldn't have cared, if she'd known who was there. Is it Alzheimer's?"

"Dementia of some sort. That's all I know."

"And you didn't diagnose what was happening to her. Fine doctor you are. And you're criticizing me. You're the one entrusted with her medical care."

"I have to go."

"You'll be hearing from me again." She ended the call and put the phone on the desk. "He's a jerk."

"I gathered that from your side of the conversation. And don't feel guilty about not coming back sooner. She turned you away when you needed her."

"I'd like to do what I can now, to make her more comfortable. I don't think she was ever happy. She was always sour and angry and combative."

"How about trying the lawyer now? We still have more people to talk to."

Sabrina picked up the phone again. "He accused me of coming back for my inheritance."

"Now that's an angle we haven't looked at. I guess we were assuming that Riley is a small town where someone with money wouldn't live. What if you're in her will?"

"She hated me."

"Do you know if she had a lot of money?"

"No. But she never worked a job. So she had an income of some sort. But she could pinch a penny till it squeaked."

"Sometimes rich people are the biggest misers. Maybe we can find out something from her lawyer."

She shifted in the chair. Then punched in the lawyer's number from her list. "This is Sabrina Walters. I need an appointment with Mr. Pendergraf to discuss my grandmother's affairs, since he's her lawyer."

"I can give you an appointment for two weeks from now."

"That's not acceptable. I'm here in town for a limited amount of time. I need to talk to him as soon as possible."

"Mr. Pendergraf is very busy. Call back in a couple of days, and I'll see if there's any cancellations."

"Could he spare me a few minutes on the phone today?"

"That's not possible."

"I'll call back tomorrow morning. I need to see Mr. Pendergraf, while I'm here." She ended the call. "I could see him in two weeks."

"That's outrageous. You did a good job. Just the tone you needed."

"Thanks for the coaching. I never would have known what to say if you hadn't given me instructions while we were on the plane."

"We could make a criminal case out of your grandmother's care. Report it to the authorities."

She shook her head. "What I want for her now is death with dignity when her time comes."

"Then we need to find someone willing to check up on her every day."

"So we need to add that to our list for today." She hesitated. She hadn't told Rafe everything that the doctor said.

"Okay, what's troubling you now? I can see it in your face."

"You're too good of a detective. Yes, something is bothering me. I was hoping we could find out about her finances from the lawyer. And not have to talk to the banker."

"What about the banker?"

She looked down at the desk. Not wanting to meet Rafe's eyes. "Dr. Atkins said that Mr. Hornsby's bank has Granny's checking account. And Mr. Pendergraf signs the checks that go out."

"What are you not telling me about the banker?" His tone was demanding. She looked up and his expression also demanded the truth.

Her heart sank. She'd hoped to keep at least some of her secrets. "Mr. Hornsby's son is the father of my baby." She said it quietly, not wanting to admit it, even then.

"Does Mr. Hornsby know that?"

"Yes. He didn't care. Told me to get out of his house." She raised her chin.

"Then what did you do?"

"I went to the county health department and they referred me to the social worker who was supposed to help teens in trouble."

"Was she the one who drove you to that home where you were coerced into giving up your baby?"

"Yes." Another quiet word.

"We need her name and we need to find out if she's still around."

"Janet Littleton, in the county social services department."

"I'll get Doug on her trail. Anything else I should know before we go confront Hornsby?"

"Mr. Hornsby wouldn't believe me when I told him Robert raped me, that he wouldn't stop when I told him to."

"Hornsby will definitely be hostile. Before we go to the bank, I'll call Doug and tell him about the social worker. What she did was criminal."

Rafe took out his cell phone and paced to the window. And quickly brought Doug up to date with what they had found out.

Then Rafe laughed and smiled widely. "Thanks. I'll get back to you when I know more. Let me know how the raid comes out." He ended the call.

"What raid?"

"Doug called the FBI. The house has been on their radar. It's still in business and selling newborns on the black market. The FBI plans a raid in the near future to seize records."

Her heart soared. "Is there a chance we can find out who has my baby?"

"Maybe. Depends on how careful they were and whether or not they thought they'd be caught someday."

"So they might not have kept the records?"

"It's possible. Don't get your hopes up."

"I want to see my Gracie again." The ache in her heart threatened to suffocate her. The same ache that developed every time she allowed herself to think about her darling baby girl. And how she'd held her in her arms for three days before she was ripped away from her. For three days she'd known unconditional love.

And now she had to face her baby's grandfather. The man who'd called her a whore.

CHAPTER 10

*R*afe sensed the waves of tension coming off of Sabrina as they walked the three blocks to the red brick building that housed the bank. She'd been subdued ever since she'd found out Phillip Hornsby's bank held her grandmother's account.

She did tell him Hornsby's son was the father of her child. Someday she might trust him enough to tell him more of her closely guarded secrets.

Rafe had made the appointment with Hornsby, so the man didn't know Sabrina was coming. The surprised look on his face was worth it. Rafe closed the office door after they were both inside. Hornsby frowned and stayed seated behind his desk.

"What are you doing here?" Mr. Hornsby launched his attack on Sabrina. "Why'd you come back to Riley?" His tone was sneering and demeaning.

"To see my grandmother." Her words were quiet. She sat in one of the chairs in front of the desk.

"And who are you?"

"Rafe Campbell. I made the appointment. I'm her escort on this trip." He used his most brusque and official sounding tone. He hated seeing her intimidated by such a man. Instead of sitting, he stood by her chair. The better to intimidate in return.

Hornsby fastened his gaze on Sabrina. "Why didn't you stay with your grandmother? So she could help you raise your brat?"

"Because she kicked me out of the house. She told me she wasn't raising another bastard." She stared at Hornsby until he turned away.

"You tried to trap my son into marriage. Getting yourself pregnant."

"You've got that all wrong, Mr. Hornsby." Her voice was still quiet but Rafe sensed the steel developing underneath.

"Robert treated me nice. No one else did. I trusted him. And he betrayed that trust. He told me I could hide out in the old barn on your property any time I wanted to."

"Trespassing, huh?"

"With your son's permission." Rafe's voice was almost a growl.

Mr. Hornsby slouched in his chair. Intimidated.

"I hid from Nathan when my grandmother wasn't home. Everyone knew Nathan was mean to me. Robert told me I didn't have to be afraid, that he'd let me hide in the barn. Then he started coming out to the barn to talk to me when he knew I was there."

"So, what were you promising him?"

Sabrina glared at Hornsby. "I was only fifteen years old. I didn't promise him anything. He took. One day he insisted on sex. I told him no. He pinned me to the floor and I screamed. He put one hand over my mouth and ripped at my clothes with his other hand. He was stronger than I was and he was on top. I had no chance. He raped me." She almost shouted the last words.

"You're lying."

"Why didn't you go to the police?" Rafe wanted the additional information out in the open.

"They wouldn't have believed me either." She lifted her chin, emphasizing her words.

Rafe moved closer to Hornsby's desk. "So Robert got away with rape. Sabrina found out she was pregnant, her grandmother kicked her out. Then a social worker took her to a place out of state where her newborn baby was taken from her and sold on the adoption black market." He let all of his anger leek into his words.

"More lies. Get out of my bank." His tone indicated he was shaken by that last revelation.

"No. I came here to ask you a simple question. Not for your insults." Some of her spunk showed again. "My grandmother has an account in this bank. Right?"

"What if she does?"

"Then you have the answers I need."

He hesitated. "All I can say is some money of hers is in the bank. Obviously you got that information from somewhere. Her lawyer signs her checks and pays her bills."

"Enough to pay for a better nursing home for her?" Sabrina sat up straight.

"I can't tell you that. Her estate is in a trust, set up by Joseph Pendergraf's father. Joseph Pendergraf manages it and controls it. All I have in my bank is her checking account. And Pendergraf keeps enough money here for the checks he writes."

"At least Nathan doesn't have control of her money." Sabrina's tone told Rafe she was worried about that possibility.

"Mrs. Walters never would have trusted Nathan." Hornsby

leveled his gaze at Sabrina. "Did you come back to find out if you're getting an inheritance?"

"No. And you're the second person who has accused me of that."

"Why did you come back?"

"I told you. To see my grandmother. I found out she was in a nursing home."

Rafe sat in the chair next to Sabrina so his eyes were on the same level as Hornsby's. He kept his gaze tight on Hornsby. "Mrs. Walters is dying in a filthy bed in a substandard nursing home." He paused, watching the expression on Hornsby's face.

"Her doctor was surly and uncooperative, insisting she was getting good care, when we could plainly see she wasn't. Her lawyer is unavailable for two weeks. Nathan is on vacation. And you are surly and argumentative."

"Who are you accusing of what?" Hornsby's words were shaky.

"Just saying something is rotten in Riley." Rafe waited.

"Nathan can't afford a vacation." Hornsby almost snarled. "He gambles away most of the money he gets. It's a wonder he still has a job."

Nathan had a gambling problem. Rafe filed that information away for future use.

Rafe stood. "I'm sorry we came to you. Obviously you won't help us."

"Why are you involved in this? Are you her boyfriend?" Hornsby's face showed his frustration.

Rafe wanted to tell him he was a private detective and Sabrina's bodyguard, but he wasn't licensed in Oklahoma and couldn't get information except in an informal way. "I told you. I'm her escort on this trip so she doesn't have to travel alone." He used his most business-like tone.

He opened the door and Sabrina followed him through the bank and out the door. Once on the street, Rafe stopped.

Sabrina looked up at him. "That didn't help."

We do know more than we did. Pendergraf has complete control of her money. It's in a trust. Pendergraf won't talk to you. Like I told Hornsby. Something is rotten in Riley."

SABRINA FOLLOWED Rafe out of the diner after their quick stop for lunch.

"We've picked up a tail. Don't turn around to look."

"What do you mean?" She kept her eyes rigidly forward.

He kept walking and she stayed by his side. "A police cruiser was in the bank parking lot when we came out. And now it's behind us, parked at the curb."

"Are you sure?" Panic rose inside her.

"Yeah. The officer is sitting there, watching us."

"Why?"

He laughed. "Intimidation. At least that answers one question. Whether or not the local police will help us."

"Now what do we do?"

"We'll go see Mrs. Murphy and see what she can tell us."

"Is that safe?"

"Relax. The officer can't do anything but follow us. We haven't broken any laws."

"Okay." They reached the grocery store. The old wooden building hadn't changed. Except for a fresher coat of paint, of the same color of light brown as it was when she'd left. The store occupied an entire short block, including parking lot. The entrance was at the side. Rafe opened the door for her.

Stepping inside, Sabrina breathed in the familiar smells that immediately transported her back to her childhood. The baked goods, the sweetness of the fruits, the mustiness of an old building. This store had been one of her sanctuaries when she was young. Mrs. Murphy had never minded when she came in to hang out instead of going home.

And Mrs. Murphy was in her usual place behind the counter. Looking a bit older, gray mixing in with the brown of her hair, but she was still the same wiry little woman who'd been one of her few friends.

Mrs. Murphy looked at her oddly, like she recognized her yet wasn't sure.

"Hi, Mrs. Murphy." Sabrina smiled and approached the counter.

"Lordy lordy, it's little Sabrina all grow'd up." Mrs. Murphy came out from behind the counter and gathered Sabrina into a big hug. Sabrina hugged her back. The warmth of her greeting helped to melt away some of the negativity she'd experienced that morning.

"You came to see your granny, didn't you?" Mrs. Murphy looked at her with sad eyes. "That poor dear. She doesn't know anyone anymore."

"She's not getting good care where she is. They aren't keeping her clean or changing her bedding regularly."

"Oh, I didn't think about that happening. I'll go check in on her regularly, but at different times so they won't know when I'm coming. I'll make sure they take good care of your granny."

"Would you? I'd be ever so grateful. I live in Oregon and I'll be going back tomorrow evening."

Mrs. Murphy looked up at Rafe by her side. Rafe extended his hand. "Mrs. Murphy. I'm Rafe Campbell, here with Sabrina to find out how her grandmother is doing."

"And we're also wondering where Nathan went on his vacation. He's not here." Sabrina kept her expression neutral.

Mrs. Murphy raised her brows in surprise. "That lazy no good. How can he afford a vacation?"

"You're the second person who's said that." Rafe also kept his tone neutral.

"He isn't having money problems, is he?" Sabrina tried for a curious tone.

"He never has any money. Spends it on booze and gambling, from what I've seen and heard. And he bought an old shack on a lake and calls it his fishing retreat. That lake ain't bigger than a little pond. He doesn't buy much groceries." She moved closer, like she had a secret to share. "Your grandmother wouldn't give him a dime. She knew his ways."

"Was she good about handling her own money?" Rafe stepped closer, keeping his voice down.

Mrs. Murphy laughed. "She was an old skinflint. Never spent much, and questioned the price of everything she bought in here. And I know she has money. Her father left it to her. That's why she never had to work."

Sabrina wrinkled her brow into a frown. "Oh, she never told me that."

"I knew her father, Oswald Benning, when he was still alive. God rest his soul. He made his fortune in the railroads as an executive. Saved all his money, then put it in a trust for his only daughter. Since his wife was long gone. And your granny's husband died real young, leaving her with two young girls to raise."

Sabrina glanced at Rafe. He had a neutral expression on his face, though she was certain he was taking mental notes.

"I've got a customer. I need to go back to the register." Mrs. Murphy moved behind the counter.

"I have a couple more questions. We'll wait." Sabrina stepped aside. Rafe did too.

Mrs. Murphy rang up groceries for two customers, then came back from behind the counter. "Now, what else do you want to know?"

"Where's Robert Hornsby these days? Did he stay in town?" She kept an innocent look on her face.

"Oh my no. He got himself in big trouble. He's in prison."

"For what?" Rafe's expression grew solemn.

"He raped a young woman from the next town and she told her parents."

Sabrina's heart clenched. He got caught. She glanced at Rafe, at his angry scowl.

"How long did he get?" Rafe controlled the anger in his voice, but she knew him well enough to know it was there.

"Seven years. He'll be out in two more years."

Sabrina's heart pounded in a staccato rhythm. That hypocrite father of his. He didn't believe her. But somebody believed another young girl.

She took deep breaths to calm her rapid heart rate. Then glanced at Rafe.

Rafe smiled, but she could tell it was a forced smile. "One more question. Do you know what kind of car Nathan drives?"

"That old Mr. Nickerson's 1982 Ford Fairlane. He sold it to Nathan when he had to stop driving. But Nathan doesn't take care of it like Joe Nickerson did. The brown paint is all chipped."

"Thank you, Mrs. Murphy. You've been a big help." Another bit of information verified.

"Nice to see you, Sabrina. You're lookin' real good." She hugged her again then glanced at Rafe, clearly curious about him. Then she glanced at Sabrina's hand, like she was checking for a wedding ring.

Sabrina felt warm fuzzies. Rafe belonging to her? It felt good to know that someone thought he could. Mrs. Murphy hadn't dismissed the idea.

"I'm glad you're still doing well and have your business." Sabrina smiled. "Some things haven't changed around here."

"You come back again, and we'll chat some more."

"I'd like that." Sabrina followed Rafe out of the store, then stopped on the sidewalk in front of the display window.

"We should have come here first." Rafe's laugh was rueful. "She gave us some valuable leads. And we now know for sure what car Nathan's driving. I'm still wondering why Pendergraf doesn't want to talk to you. We'll try once more tomorrow morning."

"Could there be a will? Could I be named in her will?" She let the disbelief through in her words.

"Her money is in a trust, even Hornsby said so. A will would specify how her estate is to be distributed at her death." He frowned. "If you and Nathan are both named in the will, it could be Nathan wants all the money."

Her heart clenched so tight she could hardly breathe. "So he decides to kill me? Comes all the way to Portland?" Her words were shaky and full of disbelief.

"That's the only thing that makes sense. But, and here's the problem, Nick needs proof that it was Nathan who put that poison in the water bottle."

"Now what do we do?"

"Check at the feed store and see if anyone knows where Nathan went on vacation. As his cousin, you can ask that question. Nick said he'd check on the sodium fluoroacetate."

"You can't ask any questions about the poison?"

"No. That would be going too far. I've already stepped over the line with Hornsby, but I couldn't resist rattling him." He sobered. "I don't want to lose my Oregon PI license."

Guilt soared through her. "No, you can't lose your license over my problems."

"I'll be careful."

They crossed the street and walked the two blocks to the feed store and went in. Sabrina glanced around, seeing two clerks. Rafe looked at her expectantly, and she shook her head. "No one I know."

"Ask that clerk at the register if Nathan is working today."

Sabrina walked up to the young clerk lounging behind the counter and smiled at him. "I'm looking for my cousin, Nathan Prescott. Is he working today?"

"Ha. He went off on a cruise he said he won in a contest. Left his wild mean dogs for me to take care of. I have to throw their food to them. I'm not going inside that fence." The clerk sneered. "And he left us to do all the work here in the store."

What work? She resisted the urge to ask.

"Thanks." She headed for the front door. Rafe steered her down the block away from the store. They stopped in front of a shoe store. She glanced at the athletic shoes displayed in the window. "We didn't do so good today, did we?"

"Think positive. We know what car Nathan drives. That he's supposed to be on a cruise he won. Highly improbable. Your grandmother will get better care from now on. And Pendergraf has something to hide."

"So what can you do about Pendergraf?"

"That Oklahoma PI I mentioned that Doug can hire. I doubt the law enforcement in this town will help."

"Oh. The cop following us."

"Yeah. I think we're seeing an example of the old boy network in this town."

"Old boy network?"

"Cronies who protect each other's back. Somebody has something to hide."

CHAPTER 11

The sun was still high in the sky, raising a sweat on his brow. Rafe glanced behind him. The police cruiser sat at the curb, a block away. "Let's head back to the motel. The police cruiser is still following us. It was in the grocery store parking lot when we came out. Now it's behind us again."

"I guess I shouldn't say this. But I've never trusted the police."

He gazed at her and frowned. "You were hassled when you were homeless?"

"Yes."

"Most police officers are honorable, but not all. We'll find out more about the police chief in this town when we see him tomorrow." He started down the sidewalk, at a slow pace so Sabrina could keep up with him.

"When we get back to the motel, I'll email Doug and Nick to update them on what we know and what we don't know."

"Can they help us with anything from out there?"

"Nick can locate a picture of a brown 1982 Ford Fairlane

sedan and put out a BOLO on it. So all the officers in Portland will be looking for the car."

"I hope they catch him." Strong, angry words.

"I do too. The trip to the police station tomorrow is probably a waste of time, but we'll go anyway. At least we're finding out who our enemies are."

"That old boy network you mentioned." A statement, not a question.

"Yeah. The chief may be part of it. Hence that cop tailing us. And not trying to hide."

"The intimidation." Sabrina increased her pace.

"No need to rush. One more block and we're there."

At the door to his room, Rafe stopped and glanced back. "I hope the cop in the cruiser doesn't get too bored." But his mind wasn't on the cop. He'd be spending hours inside the motel. With Sabrina. He'd have to tamp down his growing interest in her.

Sabrina peeked around him. "Maybe he's going to stay a block away."

Rafe unlocked the door with the card key and stepped aside to let Sabrina in. And resisted the urge to touch her as she passed him.

Once inside the room, he stopped. "Damn. I should have let you in your own door and come in here by myself. I wasn't thinking. I'm sorry."

Sabrina laughed softly and shook her head. "My reputation can't get any worse."

"Yeah. I'm betting everyone in the old boy network knows why you left. Hornsby is enough of an SOB to have told them."

"Don't worry. I don't care. I'm not coming back after Granny dies."

"I don't want you hurt." And he meant that, deep down.

"Thank you. For everything you're doing. I couldn't have faced these people alone. And I needed to see Granny while she's still alive." She gazed at him.

And he saw something in her eyes. Something he hadn't seen before. She was beginning to trust him. Maybe even like him. That was dangerous. "You've done good today. You stood up for your grandmother and for yourself." He backed away from her.

"At least I helped her. Now I'm going into my room and turn on my computer and work on a design I started." She fled through the adjoining door and closed it.

She'd felt it too.

He reached into his suitcase and took out his own computer and turned it on. Then he stood where he was, staring at the closed door. He was beginning to care too damn much for her.

Don't go there. You've been burned enough for a lifetime.

SABRINA ENDED the call and set her cell phone on the Formica table between them. "No luck. The receptionist said he had to make an emergency trip out of town." She ate the last bite of sausage on her plate, then picked up her coffee, glancing at Rafe over the rim.

Rafe sat across from her in the booth at the diner, nothing left on his plate. "Since I'm a suspicious person by nature, I suspect that Pendergraf is avoiding you. The big question is why." He frowned, that wry frown that indicated he was working a puzzle. "Pendergraf may not realize you have lots of help."

"Doug's agency and an Oklahoma PI?"

The waitress appeared and refilled their coffee cups, then took their empty breakfast plates.

Rafe waited until she'd disappeared into the kitchen. "Yes, Doug can hire an Oklahoma PI who can ask the questions I can't. And get into places I can't. We're not getting enough answers. The PI can arrange for a forensic accountant to go over Pendergraf's finances."

"Could Pendergraf be stealing from Granny? And that's why he won't talk to me?"

"One possibility. We'll find out." He laughed. "That's the one thing that does make sense. Since he's refusing to talk to you."

"So all we have left to do is the appointment with the police chief. I'd like to go back to the nursing home, look in on Granny one more time." She hesitated. "And I want to go to Granny's house, where I grew up." She'd finally made up her mind.

"We can do that. Shall we start with the house? We have time before our appointment."

She froze. Was she ready to face that house, with so many memories? "Yes." She had to.

Rafe drove down a narrow, unpaved street near the edge of town.

"That dirty white one with the fence falling down." Sabrina stared at the home where she'd spent her first fifteen years. "This used to be a nice house."

"Doesn't look like it now." Rafe stopped in front of the once white picket fence. "It could use a good paint job. And some extra nails in the fence."

"Nathan wouldn't take care of it." She pointed to the house to the left. "That's his house. Look how run down it is too."

They got out of the SUV and Nick walked toward Nathan's

house. "No car parked outside. I'll alert Nick later. Further indication the car is in Portland with him."

Nathan's two dogs started barking and running the fence around the backyard. The ones the clerk at the feed store had said were wild and mean. Sabrina retreated to the front yard of Granny's house.

One was a big black mutt with teeth bared. Looking every bit like a guard dog. Probably a German shepherd mix. The other a smaller brown mutt with at least some pit bull in him.

Rafe backed up. "I wouldn't want to be in there with those dogs. They're vicious. He climbed the stairs to the porch of Granny's house and tried the door. "Locked." He looked at her. "Who would have a key, other than Pendergraf?"

"There used to be a key outside the back door. For me." Sabrina led the way around the back, using the paving stones at the edge of what used to be a green lawn. She pulled aside a big rock near the porch. "It's still there. Did she think I'd be back?" Her heart did a flip flop.

"Were the doors always locked?"

"Not usually. But she put the key there for me, just in case. Maybe Nathan didn't know about this key."

"So she was thinking about your safety at times?"

"Maybe. I never knew with her. She was so strict and always scowling at me."

She stared off through the trees. At the weathered old barn beyond the rail fence. Her heart clenched. "That's the barn."

"Where you hid?"

"Yes." Where she'd gotten pregnant. She shuddered and turned away. She wanted her daughter back.

She unlocked the back door and peeked inside. Everything looked familiar. "It looks like someone still lives here." She stepped into the kitchen and gazed around. Her heartbeat accelerated.

She walked through the kitchen into the dining room. The buffet still had dishes on display behind the glass. "The silver tea set is gone. I wonder if she packed it away?"

Rafe ran a finger over the oak dining table. "There's no dust on the floor or the furniture. Pendergraf must be paying someone to come in and clean."

"You're right." She laughed, a delighted laugh as she saw the irony of the situation. "She must have ordered Pendergraf to keep it clean, when she went into the nursing home." She sobered, memories crowding in. "She always made me keep things dusted when I was growing up. She liked a clean house. It's sad, seeing this old house. It's in need of repairs outside. But the inside seems okay. I guess she lived here until five years ago."

"That's what Erik told us."

Sabrina wandered through rooms of overstuffed furniture, tables piled with magazines. The same egg-shell painted walls, and sheer curtains the same shade hanging at the windows. Fifteen years and nothing had changed.

Her heart ached for what might have been. She climbed the stairs. Her bedroom was at the end of the hall. The room where she'd cried. Her room, where she hadn't been safe from Nathan.

Rafe followed her, giving her space, yet being there for her protection.

Her heart pounded at a staccato rhythm. She stopped at the door. Did Nathan leave anything behind that was her? She turned the knob but the door didn't open. "It's locked. I didn't know there was a key." If she'd have known, her room could have been her sanctuary.

"Don't worry." Rafe took a small knife out of his pocket.

With a jab and a twist, he popped the lock. "These old locks are easy to get past." He pushed open the door.

She stepped into the room and the air rushed out of her lungs. "It's exactly the way I left it." The small bed where she'd slept still covered with the handmade quilt. Bathed in a ray of sunlight. Three stuffed bears on a high shelf that Nathan hadn't yet destroyed. Two pair of jeans and several shirts still on the bed. All the things that hadn't fit in her small suitcase. She picked up a blue paisley blouse and clutched it to her chest.

"Granny cared."

She dropped the blouse on the bed, smiling and crying at the same time. "She knew."

She glanced at Rafe. Big, strong, gentle Rafe had tears in his eyes.

RAFE GUIDED Sabrina down a small flight of steps to the entrance of the police station. He opened the door and the old-building musty smell assaulted him. Two pertinent questions hung over them. Would this small police department help him get the information he needed? Or would the old boy network in this town block the investigation?

Sabrina wore an anxious expression, eyes wide, gaze darting.

"You okay?"

"Nervous. Scared."

"Given what you've been through so far on this trip, that's understandable."

Rafe stopped at the desk, in front of a bored looking officer. "We have an appointment with the chief."

"Down that hallway, second door on the right." Curt words, no attempt to be sociable.

The door was open. The chief stayed in his padded chair, behind a scarred oak desk. A big man, burly, with graying hair at the temples. "Sit down." Brusque words. He waved toward two metal folding chairs in front of the desk.

"I'm Jack Howard, chief of police in this town." He scowled at Rafe. And you, Rafe Campbell, are going to lose your Oregon PI license if you so much as ask another question in my town. Is that clear?"

Sabrina gasped and shrunk down in her chair.

"I was hoping you'd be cooperative and take on the role of investigator in your town." He emphasized your.

"I've been warned that you've been nosing around and asking innocent people questions. What are you trying to find out?" His words were loud and demanding.

Rafe sat tall in his chair. "I'm trying to find some people willing to help Sabrina Walters with a problem that isn't of her making."

"What problem?" Again, that demanding tone. This man was obviously used to intimidating people he questioned.

He looked directly at Sabrina. "Did you come back to Riley to cause trouble? Why are you here?" His voice escalated in tone until he was almost shouting at her.

Rafe stood. "Sorry we bothered you."

Sabrina followed him out the door.

The chief called after them. "I still want to know the real reason you're here in Riley asking all your damn fool questions."

Rafe kept walking, without answering. He passed a guy wearing a detective shield on his belt and made eye contact with him. No threat in his eyes.

He escorted Sabrina outside, into the brisk April day. "Let's head for the park. I want to call Doug and let him know about the chief. Then we'll go to the nursing home.

"Could he make you lose your license?" Her voice was shaky.

"Only if Hornsby presses the issue. But I don't think he will. Robert is in prison for rape. The statute of limitations has passed. Erik checked. Robert can't be charged in your rape, but Hornsby was shielding his son, by ordering you out of his house. By not believing you. We can make trouble for Hornsby, and he knows it."

"I'm scared."

He turned the corner toward the park. "Don't worry. What I want to know is how the chief found out I have an Oregon PI license. He's doing his own snooping. But we don't know why."

"We need to leave town. Now." She was clearly upset, her tone fearful.

"We will, after we stop in at the nursing home and pick up our things at the motel."

"I'm sorry we came."

They reached the park and the shade of a giant oak tree. "I'm not. We did get information, just not what we were after. Like I told Hornsby, there's something rotten in Riley. And it's not all Nathan."

Two squirrels chased each other around the girth of the oak tree, not five feet from where Sabrina sat on a picnic bench. She liked squirrels. She saw one occasionally in Portland, but not like back here. Squirrels were everywhere. She glanced at Rafe. He stood next to another tree about the same distance away, talking to Doug on his cell phone.

He was telling Doug what happened at the police station. He ended his call and walked over to the bench and sat. "Doug said we did good, that we'd stirred things up very nicely, and to head home now. After we check on your grandmother, we'll drive to the airport in Oklahoma City. Meagan arranged for our flight home this evening."

"I'm ready to leave." She twisted her hands in front of her. "My emotions are a jumble. I don't know what to believe anymore."

"I know. It's been rough on you, seeing your grandmother like that and knowing what Nathan was planning for you. All in the name of greed."

"I don't understand why Nathan grew up hating me so much. Like I was an ant he needed to crush."

Rafe laid his arm on the picnic table and turned to face her. "What was his home life like? Did he only have a mother?"

"His father was there for a while, but his parents always fought. Maybe that's why Nathan was always so angry."

"I was angry as a boy. When my father beat my mother and whipped me with a belt."

"Oh dear. Then you understand Nathan? But you're always so kind and gentle."

He smiled and frowned at the same time. "What I don't understand is why he took his anger out on you. I guess anger does turn some people into bullies."

"And Nathan was a bully." She sighed, a deep sigh that came from the depths of her soul. He had made her childhood a living hell.

Rafe stood. "Let's go to the nursing home."

Sabrina followed him to the SUV and stayed silent on the short drive. Once in her grandmother's room, she lifted the blanket and found the bed was clean and her bedsores had been doctored and looked better.

"Now I can go back feeling like she's more comfortable." She smiled through tears. "Granny, thanks for locking Nathan out of my room." Her grandmother moved her hand toward Sabrina, as if she'd heard her. More tears stung her eyes. "Could she know I'm here?"

"Possibly. The human spirit can do wondrous things at times."

She leaned over the bed, close to the wrinkled face. "Granny, I want you to know that I forgive you for the way you treated me growing up and for making me leave because I was pregnant. I know you're sorry now." She wiped at the tears.

Granny lifted her hand again, then let it drop onto the bed. Sabrina glanced at Rafe. "She did hear me." She grasped Granny's hand and held it, while leaning closer. "I'm going back to Portland now. Let go and go in peace."

"That was a beautiful thing to say to her." Rafe wiped a tear from his cheek.

"I meant it. Every word of it." She tucked Granny's hand under the blanket.

They walked down the hall and out the door into the sunshine.

Sabrina's heart was lighter. She'd been able to make her grandmother's remaining days more comfortable.

But when she examined her heart, she had her own selfish reasons she didn't want this trip to end. It was like nothing she'd ever experienced. A man taking care of her, asking her what she wanted. Rafe was gentle and kind. A deep down wish surfaced. That he could be hers.

CHAPTER 12

*S*abrina unlocked the front door of the shop the next morning. Tension radiated across her shoulders and tightened her neck muscles. A light April shower added to the gloom of the day. What would she find inside? She pulled the door open.

Rafe followed her inside, no longer trying to stay out of sight. "Look around carefully. Anything out of place?"

She closely examined her work room. Nothing appeared disturbed. "Looks okay to me." Now she could get back to work, making her jewelry, supporting herself. She needed money coming in to pay her bills.

Rafe retrieved his laptop from the small cabinet and sat at the front of the table. He tapped some keys and opened the first file. "Now we'll see if he's been here."

Sabrina checked her list of orders and organized her trays of beads and gemstones for the necklace and earring set that was first on her list. Blues today. Sodalite and rocaille, big beads and tiny little ones. With silver bead accents.

Rafe stared at the video images. "He was here two nights ago, according to the date stamp. Come look."

Sabrina set down the bead and wire and walked around where she could see the screen. A man was climbing in the window. Rafe pulled another chair close and she sat.

The guy made sure his hood covered as much of his face as possible. As if he suspected a hidden camera. Then he went straight to her sketchpad and thumbed through it until he found whatever he was looking for. He fished a red marker out of his pocket and slashed a big red X across the page. His rage was evident. It was a definite slashing mark.

Sabrina's heart clenched. "That's Nathan." She reached across the table and grabbed the sketchpad. Found the page and gasped. "A finished sketch."

"Why is it Nathan?" He paused the video.

"That red X. Nathan did that to my sketches when we were kids. He said he'd X me out someday. He'd kill me." She shuddered and the tightness returned to her shoulders. She closed the pad so the page with the X was no longer visible.

Rafe reached out and caught her hand. "He knew we went to Oklahoma. That's retaliation."

"How did he know?" She pulled her hand away. Pure instinct.

Rafe scooted his chair back. "I'm sorry. I didn't mean to make you uncomfortable."

"I...I..."

He smiled softly. "I'll try to remember not to touch you."

She couldn't think of a reply that wouldn't make her feel worse than she did. He was trying to comfort her.

"Back to your question. He must be in contact with someone in Riley. I'll restart the video." Rafe struck a key to restart the playback.

"I'm surprised that's all he's done." She squeaked out the words. "He could have done more damage." She said it without feeling the least bit confident. They hadn't seen all the video.

"It's obvious he's a greedy person who believes he's entitled to whatever money your grandmother has left. And he has to kill you to get it. Or to get it all, if you are both in her will."

"He was always a bit unstable. Doing things to bring attention to himself. Kicking cats to get a rise out of people. And threatening violence." Sabrina went back to her side of the table. To put distance between herself and Rafe. She liked being close to him. And that scared her.

"He grew up without a conscience." Rafe looked across the table at her.

"I guess you could say that. He didn't care what other people thought about him, except Granny. He wanted her to like him and believe him." She picked up her needle nose pliers and twisted the wire to secure the first blue bead.

"He put something else in the refrigerator. Must be trying the poison again. He has to know you're not dead."

"I wonder who would tell him what we did in Oklahoma." Sabrina put down the small pliers she was working with and counted out six more of the blue beads. She laid them out, then looked at them, judging the symmetry.

"We'll find out." Rafe's words were emphatic. "He left after closing the refrigerator. He glanced up at the camera. See if you can identify the half face image. I'll stop it for you."

Sabrina got up and went around the table and stood behind Rafe. "Sit down so you're closer to the screen." He scooted his chair so he wasn't touching her. "Take a long, hard look. Does anything about him look familiar?"

She leaned forward, squinting at the screen. "The jut of his jaw. He's not good looking. He was always skinny and had angular features. Seems to be the same now."

"So, it does look like him? What you remember?"

"Yes. It's him. And the red X on the drawing clinches it for me."

"Still not enough to put him away for a long time." Rafe went back to the refrigerator and opened the door. "Only one water bottle is open. We don't actually have him on video pouring that vial into the bottle. And there's no way of tying him directly to the poison."

"I want this over with." She went back to her seat behind the table and picked up her pliers.

"We'll need a confession from him to convict him."

"You'll never get it. He'll lie till the day he dies. Lies come easy for him."

"Well, we can't let him kill you, in order to convict him." His tone and laugh caught Sabrina off guard.

Humor from Rafe. She liked the sight of him smiling and more relaxed. He'd been uptight the entire time they were in Oklahoma.

The bell on the front door clanged. Sabrina hurried out front, expecting her first customer of the day. Rafe followed.

Doug and Nick stood in the area in front of the counter. "How was the trip home?" Doug leaned on his cane.

"Tiring." Rafe's one-word answer said it all.

Sabrina nodded. "I agree. I'd never flown before. The plane was crowded and noisy and the airport was pure chaos."

Doug laughed. "Welcome to the real world."

She shrunk back.

His expression was apologetic. "I meant it as a joke, not a criticism of how you live your life. I admire what you've done and how much you've accomplished on your own."

She relaxed a bit. Still leery. She never knew what to expect from Doug.

"So, anything more to report today?" Nick gestured toward the back. "Before we tell you the good news."

"How about the good news first?" Rafe laughed. "We need something to cheer us up."

"That bad?" Doug chuckled. "I need to sit. Let's go to the back."

Sabrina returned to her chair behind the work table. The men sat on the other three wooden chairs in the room.

Doug looked straight at Rafe. "You two riled up a lot of people in Riley. I got a call from Oklahoma before you two were even in the air. A police detective, name of Mike Pearson. He overheard your conversation with the chief."

Rafe pushed the laptop away. "The guy we passed in the hallway on the way out. He made eye contact with me. Like he wanted to say something but couldn't."

"So how did the detective link you to me? Why did he call me?" Doug's expression was puzzled.

"The chief knew I was an Oregon PI and threatened to have my license pulled."

"So Pearson found out where you worked from the state licensing bureau and called me. He told me the county district attorney is investigating the chief for other misdeeds Pearson couldn't mention."

"Ah. The plot thickens." Rafe laughed.

Nick took over the narrative. "Doug gave him my number, since I'm doing the investigation here. I let him know what's going on and he'll keep looking for the source of the sodium fluoroacetate and get any information that will help us tie Nathan to the poison."

Sabrina sat back and relief flooded her. Going to Oklahoma had been a good thing. Nick and Rafe had help.

"So he's going to be in contact with you?" Rafe looked directly at Nick.

"Yes. I'm his Oregon connection."

"Now for the bad news." Doug gestured toward the laptop.

Rafe hit a key and activated the screen, then pushed the laptop down the table where both Doug and Nick could see it. Then started the video. "Here he comes."

They watched in silence, studying every move the culprit made from the time he pushed the window open.

Doug pushed back in his chair and looked at her. "Can you identify him from that half shot?"

"Yes. The jawline is distinct."

"Good. At least we have that." Nick sounded pleased.

"And that red X on her drawing. He's done that before." Rafe backed it up to that section.

Sabrina opened her sketchbook and removed the disfigured sheet and handed it to Nick. "Maybe you can use that as evidence."

"Does the red X mean anything to you?" Doug seemed puzzled.

"When Nathan did that to my drawings, he told me he was going to X me out someday. Kill me."

"That's a warning for you, Rafe. Keep her safe." Doug's tone was almost threatening. "You'll have to stick with her all day. Alison had to go to court over that arson case. She'll be tied up during the day till it's over."

"And Kara?"

"Still working that insurance fraud case in San Francisco."

Then Doug turned to her. "I have some other news for you.

The FBI raided that house in Kansas and seized the records. The FBI is trying to trace all the babies who were sold on the adoption black market."

Sabrina's heart raced. "Does that mean I may be able to find my daughter?"

"Maybe." Doug looked straight at her. "Don't get your hopes up too high. The records may not be complete. We don't know what the FBI found. They don't keep local police departments informed."

Maybe get Gracie back? She could hardly believe it was possible. "So, what happens now?" Sabrina pointed to the laptop. "Do I simply keep on working and waiting for Nathan to do something besides break in here and try to poison me?" She couldn't keep the panic out of her voice.

Nick took out his cell phone and told dispatch to send the crime scene expert to the shop. "We have to check everything in the refrigerator again. At least there's not as much to check this time. And he wore those plastic gloves. No prints."

"We put in fresh food and drinks, like Doug said." She used her don't-cross-me tone like a shield the way she'd used a bucket to ward off an attack by Granny's rooster.

"You're doing good." Doug smiled at her.

She glanced at him, but couldn't smile. Doug and Nick and Rafe were so used to being police and doing things their way. It made her uncomfortable at times. Most of the time, if she were honest.

Doug stood. And limped toward the back door. "I'll go out this way. I didn't think about it when we came in. I hope we weren't seen by Nathan."

"He has to know something is going on," Nick said. "I'll stay and let the expert in and watch what he does this time." He turned to Rafe. "Take her back home or out for coffee or what-ever. I'll text you when we're ready to go."

Sabrina sighed. Ordered out again. Ordered around by the big men who wanted to protect her. When she needed to work. Serious stuff, being the target of a murderer. That red X meant Nathan still wanted to kill her.

CHAPTER 13

*R*afe held the front door open for her. "Let's head for the cafe. Coffee and a maple bar sounds good to me."

"Okay." Hesitation and one quiet word.

"Or would you rather go back to your house?"

"The cafe." More hesitation. She seemed upset but trying not to show it. She had plenty to be upset about.

Rafe walked toward the cafe down the street. Sabrina kept pace with him, despite the difference in the lengths of their strides. He admired her energy.

He admired too much about her. This case needed to end before he did something foolish like fall in love with a beautiful young woman who needed more than he could give.

He opened the door of the cafe and followed Sabrina in. They stopped at the counter and Sabrina chose a cream puff and he picked the maple bar. Then they took the booth in the corner. A waitress brought them coffee and their pastries.

After the waitress left the table, Sabrina scowled instead of eating her cream puff. Her usual sunny expression replaced by a dour one.

"What's wrong?" He kept his words gentle.

"I want my normal life back. I want to be able to run my business. I want to do the things I like to do." She sighed. "I'm tired of being afraid and wondering what Nathan will do next."

He took a bite of his maple bar and chewed it. "I know. It's tough having your life turned upside down by someone you assumed you'd never see again."

"Yeah. I hadn't thought about him in a while. It's like he couldn't stand not bugging me and had to come back into my life to bug me some more. His sadistic side."

She took a bite of her cream puff and her eyes lit up. And she almost smiled. Then she took a sip of her coffee and put it down. And scowled again.

"Why did Nathan put something else in the refrigerator? He must realize the first time didn't work, that no one actually drank the water? And if he did put more poison in, why would he leave the X that shows me he was back? He's not being logical."

"If he's a true sociopath, and I think he is, then what he does doesn't have to make sense to anyone but him. He lives by his own rules."

"He's always been that way. I guess he didn't change when he grew up."

"True sociopaths don't change."

"I hope he's caught soon." She picked up her coffee cup and took a sip, her scowl back as she watched him over the rim. "What happens now?" Frustration leaked through her words.

A man in her house and in her shop. A cousin wanting to

kill her. Always people around telling her what to do. No wonder she was frustrated.

"I'd like to be able to tell you that the police will pick up Nathan and put him in jail and you'll never see him again. But life doesn't work like that."

"Yes. Life is messy sometimes. I just want it all to go away."

"Nick is looking at all the angles. He has others in the department working with him. Police work is exacting and time consuming. They have to build a solid case against Nathan."

"Then I guess I need to be patient." She let out a big sigh. "I hate sitting around waiting for something else to happen."

"I know. At least now we know it's Nathan and not someone else. Nathan knew you in a way no one else ever did. Am I right?"

"If you mean, he knew how to push my buttons, yes."

"Pushing buttons is a useful thing to do if you want to frustrate someone and get them under your control. You see, he did control you. You told me you couldn't go home until your grandmother was there. And she was gone many afternoons."

"And Nathan took advantage of that."

She picked up her cream puff and finished it off. He took the last bite of his maple bar, then sipped his coffee.

"I've been thinking. I need to leave now. Before he kills me."

"And miss your chance to get your daughter back?"

She gasped. "Oh. I can't leave. I want her back."

"Doug is doing all he can to find her. Trust him. Trust Nick and the police department."

She wiped at her chin with her napkin. "So, what do I do? Wait until Nathan comes back and we find out what he plans?"

"You won't be alone. You'll have someone armed with a gun with you at all times."

"And that's supposed to make me feel safe? Nick said that poison would have killed me within six hours. It was pure luck the camera was in place when he decided to use the poison."

"You're right about that. Had he used the poison the first time he broke into your shop, you would have died and no one would have known what was going on or why."

"Why didn't he? Why did he play around so I'd know who was doing it? Was it his ego? He wanted me to know why I was dying?"

"Not that you'd think about that when you were passed out from the poison."

"It doesn't make sense."

"No, it doesn't. We need to look closer at his background and find out what he's been doing these past fifteen years."

"He's still working the job he had when I left Riley."

"That tells us something about his motivation to get ahead in the world. He didn't marry either, I guess. We're assuming he doesn't have a wife. But he could have a girlfriend."

"It's possible. Though he was as much of a loner as I was when we were young. He didn't have friends so he entertained himself tormenting me."

The outer door opened and Rafe glanced up. It was Nick. He spotted them and headed their way. Rafe scooted over so Nick could sit next to him. Sabrina let out a sigh of relief. She was still afraid of big men.

"Doug said I'd probably find you here."

"Do you have news?" Rafe asked.

"Not on the poison yet, though the crime scene has been cleared. Nathan was traced to a motel in southeast Portland, but he moved out last night, before the officers got there."

"He's spooked now."

"I think someone in Oklahoma told him you'd been back

there asking questions. So he still has a friend or contact in Riley."

"That's what we decided," Rafe said. "Though we don't know who it is."

"That coffee smells good. And you had a pastry to go with it." He signaled the waitress and she came and took his order. "Back to business. But I couldn't ignore my sugar craving."

Rafe laughed.

"So he knows his poison didn't work and we're onto him." Nick's words were grim.

"He was bound to get wise to what we're doing, if he's watching the shop."

"We have patrols out now looking for anyone loitering around, or looking like they're staking out either the shop or her house."

"Has anyone checked the house today, while we've been at the shop?"

"I've requested frequent patrols by the house. I'll follow up and make sure it's being done."

The waitress delivered Nick's coffee and maple bar. He took a big bite and smiled.

"What do you want us to do?" Rafe gazed at Sabrina, at the solemn expression on her face.

Nick finished chewing. "Let Sabrina go back to work and keep the shop open for now. As long as he doesn't try something that's immediately dangerous. If he comes in again, we can catch him on camera. Though I think that window should be bolted shut so he can't get in. That will frustrate him even more."

"Hold off a bit longer, until we get closer to catching him." Rafe looked at Sabrina again. "What do you want to do, besides run?"

"How do you figure out what I'm thinking?" Her tone was one of exasperation. With an undertone of anger. "I need to go back to work on the necklace I'm making."

"Run?"

"An inside joke. We've both solved problems in the past by running from them. She'd decided to stay, though she was having second thoughts until I reminded her Doug could find her daughter for her."

Nick arched a brow. Rafe gave a quick shake of his head. No involvement, it signaled. Nick smiled slightly. Got the message.

Now Rafe had to stick to his resolve. It was getting harder each day. Shy little Sabrina was prodding more than his protective urges.

SABRINA ADJUSTED the cushion behind her back. Her lumpy couch wasn't the best place to work on her designs. But Rafe was in the kitchen. He'd be setting the table for their dinner. The one flat surface in the house that was the right height.

Rafe rattled pans in the kitchen. Guilt seized her insides. Doug supplied the food. Rafe cooked it. A low-grade panic pushed out the guilt. She was never alone anymore. Her independence gone. Until Nathan was caught.

She took a deep breath and bent over the sketchpad in her lap, using her pencil to adjust the placement of the largest stone in the necklace she was designing. Redesigning. She was redoing the sketch Nathan had destroyed with the red X. The sketch she'd given Nick as evidence. Tedious mind-stretching work, but she had a good memory for her designs.

One day Nathan destroyed an entire sketchbook of her drawings of people and animals and the meandering creek that ran through Riley. Every single page slashed with red. She'd kept that sketchbook, hidden in the top of her closet, in the hopes Granny would believe her someday. It might still be there. Granny would never see if now.

A cupboard door slammed. Startling her. Rafe was usually quieter.

They'd gotten to her house late last night, from the airport. And Rafe had brought a bedroll into the house from his car. He'd slept on the floor, in that bedroll. More guilt soared through her. She stared at the closed drapes, at the bedroll under the window, abandoning her sketch. He was probably still tired from the trip, and from sleeping on the floor.

Why was Nathan in Portland, still destroying? Forcing her to share her house with Rafe? She still felt uneasy knowing she was alone with him in the house at night. Though he hadn't done anything to destroy her trust in him.

"What is it? You look worried."

She jumped at the sound of his voice. He stood in the doorway to the kitchen. She grabbed at an idea to satisfy his curiosity. "Nathan can't get my share of the inheritance unless I'm dead. If that's the way the will is written."

"So he had to find you and kill you to get all the money. And the authorities in Oklahoma have to know you're dead." Rafe sank into the chair across from her.

"So that's why he's doing what he's doing. But I can't go away and let him have the money. He'd come looking for me again."

"Yes. He would." His gaze was intense. "You have to die for his plan to work."

"I'm not going to drink his damn poison and let him have the money. He always got his way when they were kids. Not this time." She let her anger show through in her words.

Rafe laughed. "You're fighting mad now."

"If there's an inheritance, I'd like to claim my share. When Granny dies." Extra money to make her life easier. She wouldn't have to work such long hours.

"I'll help you get it." Rafe stood. "If I switched the two lamps in here, you'd have better light to work by. Since you sit on the couch to sketch." He pulled the plug on the lamp by the chair he was sitting in and moved it behind the couch, plugging it in there. Then he took the lamp she'd been using and moved it next to the chair.

"Better?"

"Better. Thanks." He was always thinking about her comfort. It scared her.

"Dinner's almost ready. I'll call you when I have it dished up." He disappeared into the kitchen.

She wished she'd learned to cook. On the streets, she ate whatever was available. Buying it when she had money or getting it from a soup kitchen.

Since moving into this house, she'd relied on canned goods or frozen dinners. Cooking looked so complicated. She'd rather spend her time making her jewelry and selling it in the shop. Her needs weren't much. Security. A roof over her head.

"Come eat."

She put down her pad and pencils and headed for the little kitchen.

When both of them were in there, they almost filled up the room. The night there were three big men in her tiny kitchen, she'd felt completely overwhelmed. That was the night she'd learned about the poison meant to kill her. The night all illusions of safety in Portland vanished.

She sat at the table and he put a plate of chicken and salad in front of her. Delicious aromas filled the kitchen. She stared at the plate.

"Now you're thinking about something else."

"I'm thinking about why Nathan is taking so many chances. If he gets caught, he won't be able to spend the money."

"Some people don't think things through, to the consequences. Some criminal types are clueless about how to go about committing their crimes without getting caught."

"I used to think he was kind of smart. I guess he isn't."

"So, what kind of future do you envision for yourself? What are your long term plans?"

"After Nathan is caught, I'll live here and work in my shop and take care of myself. I don't need much."

"No plans to find a guy and settle down and marry and have kids?"

"No. I'm not looking for a man. Besides, if I had another baby, it wouldn't be to replace my little Gracie. I hadn't really thought about having more children." She brightened. "But I hope Doug finds Gracie for me."

"You don't go out on dates?"

"No. The only men who show interest in me are looking for sex." She glanced at Rafe.

Rafe sometimes looked at her in a way that said he was interested. She'd seen that look in a man's eyes before. Did Rafe want sex with her? Did all men think of sex and nothing else?

She forked a bite of the chicken thigh on her plate, far too aware of Rafe, across the small table from her. Those tingly feelings he stirred up inside her...they scared her."

She had two choices if she wanted to stay in Portland and keep her business. And maybe get her daughter back. Two choices, both involving different kinds of danger. One to her independence, one to her life.

Rafe with her all the time. Stirring up those feelings. Or being alone and at the mercy of Nathan, not knowing whether Nathan's next move would prove deadly.

CHAPTER 14

*R*afe jolted awake. A scraping sound came from the backyard. Why wasn't the light on? He jumped up from his bed on the floor, grabbed his jeans and pulled them on, pushed his feet into his athletic shoes. No time for socks.

He crept to the back door, keeping his flashlight shielded so only a sliver of light escaped. He peered through the window. A black plastic bag covered the motion detector light. More scraping noises. Nothing in his line of sight. Then silence.

Since he was the only one on duty tonight, he had to stay in the house until backup arrived.

He went to the living room and called 911, requesting two patrol cars, no sirens. And told the dispatcher a guy in the back yard was wanted for questioning.

More scraping, then more silence. He itched to burst through the door and grab the guy. But his job was to protect Sabrina, not try to be a hero. He checked the clock in the kitchen.

The first patrol car arrived less than three minutes later,

siren blaring until he got within two blocks of the house. Rafe seethed inside.

Sabrina screamed. Rafe ran up the stairs to her room. She was sitting up in bed, wide-eyed and shaking. "What's happening?" Her words trembled.

"I heard a noise outside and called 911 and requested two patrol cars. That was the first one to arrive."

"Was it Nathan?"

"Probably. I need to go back downstairs. Stay here. You're safe."

She burrowed down in the covers. As much as he wanted to remain with her and comfort her, he couldn't.

Someone knocked on the front door. He hurried down the stairs and opened the door to an officer.

"I chased him but couldn't catch him. He hopped a fence and ran into the woods. I lost him in the underbrush."

"You didn't hear the request for no siren?" Rafe controlled his words, tamping down his anger.

"Sorry. Habit. What did the guy do?"

"That's what I want to know. I heard a scraping sound."

A second car pulled to the curb. This one came silent. Not that it made a difference now.

Rafe locked the front door and led the two officers around the house to the backyard. "Could you tell if the guy was wearing thin plastic gloves?"

"Yeah. I saw the gloves when he grabbed the top of the fence."

Rafe pulled the black plastic off the motion detector light and it came on, illuminating the entire yard. "There won't be any prints. He never leaves any."

"What's he wanted for?"

"Breaking and entering, so far, and maybe attempted murder. It's Nick Castellani's case."

Rafe gestured to a pile of leaves next to the foundation. "And now attempted arson." He stomped the leaves and extinguished one glowing ember.

One officer bent down. "It didn't light. Just a few charred leaves. Everything is still damp from the shower this afternoon."

"Thank goodness for Oregon showers. The scraping sound I heard was the guy piling up the leaves. That pile is high enough for the flames to reach the siding." Rafe's stomach knotted. "This old house is tinder dry."

He glanced at the second story window directly above the leaves. Sabrina's bedroom.

SABRINA STOPPED at the bottom of the stairs, still groggy from lack of sleep. Rafe had come to her bedroom door in the middle of the night to tell her that Nathan had got away. But that's all he said. She hadn't gone back to sleep.

Rafe was talking to someone. She found him at the kitchen table, on his cell phone.

"See you later." He ended the call.

Her curiosity gnawed at her insides. She edged into the chair on the other side of the table.

"That was Doug. I filled him in on what happened last night."

"How did Nathan get away from the cops?" She tried to gulp back a yawn, but it escaped anyway.

"He had an escape route planned, over the back fence and into the trees."

"What was he doing outside?" Though she'd wanted more

answers during the night, she hadn't gone downstairs in her nightshirt to ask. She needed a bathrobe with Rafe in the house.

"He piled leaves to set a fire, but they were too damp." He was watching her, like he didn't know what her reaction would be. Those dark eyes that saw so much.

A knot formed in her stomach. She kept her voice as steady as she could. "He did that once. Set a shed on fire with leaves. To prove to me he could do it. Then told me he'd choke me if I tattled."

"Real nice guy." A frown accompanied his sarcastic tone.

"What about the light outside?"

"He covered it with a black plastic bag."

"I was afraid the lights wouldn't work. Nathan can always figure out a way to do what he wants."

"You're still alive. He hasn't succeeded."

The knot tightened in her stomach. "But he keeps trying."

Rafe rose from the table and grabbed two skillets from a cupboard. And got bacon from the refrigerator. "Scott just finished an investigation he was doing. He's now assigned to outside surveillance, every night, all night. Starting tonight."

"Good. I don't want to be burned out of my house." Quiet yet emphatic words she felt deep down. Not now, not after she'd worked so hard for all she had.

He set the skillets on the burners and started the bacon frying in one. Then added frozen hash browns to the other.

Once he had the food cooking, he turned toward her. "You won't be burned out, if I can help it." Sincerity laced his words, yet she was unconvinced.

"Don't make a promise you might not be able to keep."

"Still don't trust me?" His half grin. The one that seemed to promise more than he said.

"You haven't stopped Nathan yet." Keep the focus on Nathan.

"The police have that job. I have the job of taking care of you." Suggestive words. To go with the intensity of his gaze. They sparked tingling sensations, like last night. Down there. Sensations that scared her.

The odor of frying bacon drifted her way. She willed her body to stay in the kitchen, not flee upstairs. He had looked at her in that all male way she'd seen many times. Yet he never did anything out of line. He was the perfect gentleman.

She slipped from behind the table. "Thanks for cooking. Again."

"I have to eat too." That crooked grin widened.

She took plates from the cupboard and set them next to the stove, then got out silverware and glasses and poured orange juice from the jug. The scent of brewed coffee reached her nose. She usually didn't bother making it for herself. She got out the cups and poured the coffee. And sat down with her cup.

In a few minutes Rafe had the two plates filled with bacon, eggs, and hash browns and had set them on the table.

He was acting normal now. The moment had passed. And she felt guilty thinking about it. As soon as Nathan was caught and put in jail, Rafe would go work on another job for Doug and she might never see him again.

"The man from the security company will be here shortly to move the motion sensor lights higher, out of Nathan's reach."

"Good. I want Nathan caught."

"We all do."

"Did you get any sleep at all last night?"

"Hardly any. Doug told me that Alison's trial ended abruptly in a plea deal late yesterday. She's coming by and she'll go to the shop with you today. I'll take a nap, then go see Doug, to talk strategy."

"You'd better sleep so you'll be thinking straight."

"Yes. I don't do well when I've lost almost an entire night's sleep."

Here they were, sitting in her kitchen, talking about silly things like sleep. As well as the man who was trying to kill her. Two weeks of weird.

What would Nathan do next?

RAFE SQUARED his shoulders and pulled open the side door of the agency. Then strolled into Doug's office. His gut coiled into a tight knot. Doug's summons, in the middle of his nap, had caught him off guard.

Doug waved him to a chair in front of the desk.

"What the hell is going on?" Doug used his strident, I-don't-like-this tone.

"You know as well as I do. Nathan is serious about killing her. I'm trying to protect her."

"Where are you sleeping?"

So that's what it's all about. "In a bedroll on the hard living room floor. The carpet is very thin. I go back to my house to shower and change clothes. That's where I was when you called. Getting some sleep." Rafe let his own frustration show.

Doug shifted in his chair. Didn't say anything. Just stared at him.

"I can't leave her alone at night. Especially after last night." Words to fill the void. But the truth. "What's the problem?"

"Alison caught the look that passed between you and Sabrina when they went out the door this morning."

Were his feelings that obvious? But Sabrina? "I repeat, what's the problem?"

"I don't want either of you hurt when this is over."

Relief sped through him. Okay. He got that. Doug was thinking about Nick and Tricia, when Nick was protecting her from that stalker. "Believe me, Sabrina would never let me get anywhere near her bed. If that's what you're worried about."

Doug steepled his fingers. "Make sure nothing does happen."

"She doesn't want to be touched." Rafe kept his gaze steady.

"Okay. Make sure you continue to keep your hands off." An ultimatum. Delivered forcefully. "Back to the other problem. Why wasn't Scott outside last night?"

"He worked late on his own case. No chance for a nap." Rafe kept his tone neutral.

"Damn. I feel like pacing. Wish I could. Might help." He glanced out the window to his left. "We should have caught Nathan last night."

"You want my gut feeling on this?" Rafe didn't wait for an answer. "The poison didn't work. Nathan is going to try fire again."

Doug swiveled his chair. "I hope you're wrong."

"I do too." His gut tightened, contradicting his words.

Meagan appeared at the door with the coffee pot and an empty cup. She refilled Doug's cup and poured one for him. Then left.

Doug took a sip, then set his cup down. "Is she okay with what we're doing for her?" Doug's strident tone was gone, replaced with a more conciliatory tone.

"She's putting up with me in the house. She wants to stay and keep her shop. She wants to keep the life she's built. She wants her daughter back."

Doug's dark eyes softened. "Nathan first, then her daughter."

"Of course."

"Another subject. Why does she carry that laptop everywhere?"

"She has all her designs on it. And records of sales. A spread-sheet for her supplies. I've watched her work. She's highly intel-ligent about how she runs her business."

"I'll send Erik to the shop today to set her up with online backup. That might ease her mind some. She doesn't strike me as one to use the latest technology."

"No. Her cell phone is an old flip phone and she uses flash drives for backup." He picked up his coffee cup.

"Get her a better phone when you can. It might mean connecting when she needs help."

"I'll check everything she's using and see where we can upgrade."

"We can't leave anything to chance." Doug narrowed his gaze. "Why would Nathan try fire?"

"Sabrina said he once started a fire in an old shed with a pile of leaves to prove he could do it."

"He must know we're looking for him. No one has spotted that old car. Nick's as puzzled as I am."

"Could be hidden somewhere. He's one determined guy."

"Sabrina ought to go on an extended vacation while we catch this guy."

"She won't. It was a huge step to reach out to Kara for help, and then to accept help from you and the rest of the group. Including me. She's still not trusting me."

"Past experience with big men?"

"I'd bet on it. The kid who raped her was probably husky, if his father's size is any indication. And she was bullied by the father." He set down his cup. "Then there were her years living on the street."

Doug raised an eyebrow. "You've been talking more. You're getting information you didn't have."

"She doesn't tell me any more than she has to. I keep prying."

Doug scrunched his eyebrows in his signature scowl. "Tonight Alison will be in the house with you and Sabrina, and Scott will be outside from eleven on. In case Nathan tries again."

So, Alison was going to be inside to protect Sabrina from him. "It wouldn't surprise me. He's done a lot in less than two weeks." He kept to the subject of Nathan and safety.

Yet keeping her safe had become more than a job in those two short weeks. Much more than a job.

RAFE JUMPED up from the chair by the front window and paced to the kitchen. The knot in his gut twisted tighter. He couldn't get interested in the movie Sabrina and Alison were watching. He couldn't sit still any longer. Every single nerve ending in his body was on alert, waving a danger flag.

He stopped pacing when Alison joined him in the kitchen.

"Why don't you go upstairs and try to nap? You're going to have a long night. You're wound up like a toy airplane ready to take flight."

He leaned against the counter. "I won't sleep tonight. Something is going to happen. I feel it in my gut."

"Is Scott here yet?"

"Doug said eleven o'clock."

She glanced at the clock on the stove. "Thirty more minutes."

"No one is sleeping upstairs tonight." His words were emphatic, decisive.

Sabrina stood at the kitchen door. "Do you think he'll try again so soon?"

Her eyes were wide pools of brown. Scared brown like the eyes of that mutt he'd once rescued. He couldn't lie to her.

"Yes."

Sabrina glanced around the kitchen. "I don't have much in this house that belongs to me. I rented it furnished. But it's home." Her words were plaintive, almost a wail.

Alison looked at him, waiting for his response.

He made his decision. "Let's go to my house. Why wait here to see what he does?"

"My backpack is upstairs."

"Go get it. And grab anything else you'll need in the next couple of days."

Alison sat at the table. "I'll stay here and watch the back of the house."

"Good idea. I'll take the front."

"I'll go fast." Sabrina left the kitchen at a run and her footsteps pounded on the stairs.

He stood in the doorway to the kitchen. "I'm sorry I spooked her like that, but it's for the best. She needs to be on the alert too."

"I think you're right. We do need to leave here." Alison moved the chair closer to the back door.

"I'll watch out the front window." He went back to the living room, then crossed to the window and peeked out the slit at the side of the drapes. Nothing going on that he could see, but he continued to scan the neighborhood.

A car turned the corner onto the street, then stopped at the second house on the other side. Not even close. He tried to relax and focus on his breathing.

A routine surveillance job.

No. It wasn't.

Sabrina was in danger.

He could not fail her. Even if she could never be his. Keeping her alive would disprove the curse he'd lived with.

She came down the stairs with her backpack and two duffel bags. And dumped them on the couch. "I got what matters. Almost."

He glanced at her, then back to the street, then her again.

She opened the backpack and stuffed in her laptop and sketch book that were sitting on the couch. Then looked around. "That's it. Maybe he won't do anything if we're gone."

"Don't count on it." He checked the street again. And tensed. Someone was moving at the side of the house. Back by the trash can. The knot in his gut tightened into a rock-solid ball. That someone ran to the front of the house and hurled what looked like a brick. For a brief moment the hooded figure was illuminated by the motion detector light.

"Holy shit!" He jumped back as the front window shattered, sending a spray of glass everywhere. Several shards nicked his arms. The drapes tumbled down. He rushed to Sabrina, and pushed her toward the kitchen. A firebomb landed on the floor in front of the couch and the entire couch exploded into a huge roaring fireball that ignited the wall and licked at the ceiling.

Sabrina screamed.

CHAPTER 15

*P*anic seized Sabrina's heart. "My backpack." She shouted above the roar of the fire engulfing the living room.

"Too late." Rafe's fingers bit into her arm, forcing her through the kitchen, away from the rapidly spreading flames. And out the back door. She stumbled on the crack in the concrete walkway and her legs buckled. Rafe grabbed her around the waist and pushed her past the burning house and across the street to the sidewalk.

He hugged her to his body, his arms like bands of steel. After a moment, he pulled his phone from his pocket, dialed 911. And gave the dispatcher the necessary information.

Sabrina was shaking and coughing, and clinging to him, burrowing into the T-shirt covering his chest. Disbelief crowded out other thoughts.

He ended his call and hugged her tighter. Kept her turned away from the house, from seeing the flames.

A deep void of emptiness shot through her. "All gone. My

money. Everything." Her words were muffled by the closeness of his chest. Tears threatened but she willed them away. Now was not the time to cry. Anger took over. A searing rage. She would not let Nathan win.

"You're alive. That's what matters." He loosened his grip.

She gasped. "You're bleeding."

He took a handkerchief from his pocket and wiped at the streaks of blood on his arms. "No deep cuts. But I got blood on your sweater."

"It will wash."

Rafe looked around. "Where's Alison?"

"She was by the back door. Surely she got out before we did." She wiggled in his arms, fighting to get her emotions under control. To behave more calmly. She'd been in tight spots before, and survived. She'd survive this.

She stared at what was left of the house. Flames torched the night sky. The house had gone up like a carton of matches. Old dry wood.

Fire engines arrived with sirens blaring and firefighters quickly unrolled hoses and attacked what was left of the fire.

Alison rounded the corner and ran toward them. She was breathing hard. "Don't know where he went. Couldn't find a trace."

"He had his escape route planned," Rafe said.

"How are you holding up, Sabrina?" Alison gazed at her, compassion filling her eyes.

"I'm okay." She broke away from Rafe's arms. And stood straight. She didn't trust herself to say any more. Her feelings were too raw.

Alison turned to Rafe. "What happened? What did I miss?"

"A brick followed by a Molotov cocktail that landed in front of the couch."

"No wonder there's nothing left." Alison's gaze shifted to her. "Your backpack was on the couch."

"Things can be replaced." Rafe's words stung.

"My emergency money was in the backpack. I can't replace that." She was sorry for the pouty tone, but it was the way she felt.

"I'm sorry. I wish you'd trusted a bank."

"I don't trust anyone but myself." She meant that on one level. She'd trusted Rafe to save her life. "Thanks for saving me." The words sounded lame even to her. If not for Rafe, she wouldn't be alive.

"Part of the job description, saving damsels in distress." He'd moved away from her, from the contact. Like he was afraid she'd panic if he got close again.

The water on the fire squelched the remaining flames, but dark smoke billowed into the night sky.

The left wall collapsed into the ruins. Sabrina jumped.

Doug limped around the corner, using his cane, and made his way to them. "Are all of you okay? I was heading this way to talk to you when Nick called me with the news."

"I'm glad you didn't get here earlier." Alison's eyes widened into alarm. And Sabrina got the message. Doug might not have made it out of the house in time.

Rafe looked around. "I haven't seen Scott. Did he come?"

"He just got here," Doug said. "He's watching from around the corner, in case our guy comes back to look at what he did."

"Good idea."

Sabrina stood silently, between Rafe and Alison. She still couldn't believe this had happened. A nightmare becoming real. Nathan had tried to kill them with fire. Had they been upstairs, they would have died. Rafe's insistence that she hurry saved her. But not the things she went upstairs to get.

Now she had to start all over. Nothing left except the shop. "Will he try to destroy the shop too?" The words came out as a whisper.

Doug gazed at her tenderly. "I hope not. Nick said there will be saturation patrols from now on."

"I have nowhere to live. No clothes. Nothing."

"We'll take care of it." Doug's I'll-handle-this tone.

"We were getting ready to go to my place. He struck early."

"That's a good idea. You do have a decent security system, don't you?"

"Yes. And he may not know where I live."

"Go ahead and take her there. For some reason he's not driving his car now." Doug frowned. "I'd like to know why."

Sabrina stared at the smoldering ruins, at the stream of water from the fire hose, at the people on the sidewalk watching. A deep sense of loss sat in the pit of her stomach. Everything gone. Completely.

"We'll continue to keep Sabrina under constant watch so he can't get to her." Doug's words showed he was in charge and approved the plan.`

Moved around like a pawn. Her little-girl-helplessness threatened to engulf her. Instead, she reached back to a time of strength, when she'd discovered Vivian had been stealing from her. She'd packed up her few belongings and boarded the next Greyhound for Portland.

But she couldn't run now. She couldn't go back on the streets to survive. She couldn't start over. She still had her shop and her ability to design jewelry. Then there was the hope she'd get her daughter back.

An ember in the ashes flared up. She'd stay and fight.

∾

RAFE DROVE FURTHER east and south, into an older residential district. The houses were bigger than the little one she'd lived in. He parked at the curb behind a dark-colored SUV, in front of a two story home on a corner lot.

Sabrina gazed at the trees, the flowers, the clean, uncluttered look. The street lamp down the block gave off enough dim light to show a nice house. Not the apartment she'd expected.

A single man with a house of his own.

Alison had gone with Doug. Her car had been blocked by fire engines and hoses. Sabrina would be alone with Rafe in his house. Not really different than being in her house with him. Yet it was different.

He locked his car and took her into the house by the front door. There didn't seem to be a garage. A lot of older homes didn't have garages. She'd discovered that since arriving in the city.

"Come on in and make yourself at home. I'll find something for you to sleep in and in the morning we'll go shopping and get you some more clothes. Since what you're wearing is all you have."

"I don't have any money to buy clothes. And my credit card and check book are gone too."

"Doug gave me a credit card he uses for clients in need. You're a client in need." He smiled at her.

She didn't like the sound of that. She'd been self-sufficient for a long time now. "I have some money in the cash register at the shop."

"Enough to replace your wardrobe?"

"I can buy a few things, to get me by. I don't keep much cash there. Most of my money was in the backpack that burned."

"Then don't worry about paying for now. We'll get you what you need."

Guilt welled up inside her. She couldn't take care of herself anymore.

"It's still the middle of the night. Let's see if we can get some sleep. Come upstairs and I'll show you to your room." He said it so matter-of-fact, as if having a stranger as a guest in his house was no big deal. She followed him up the stairs.

He pushed open the door of a small, but nicely furnished bedroom. "The bathroom is across the hall."

She stood in the middle of the room. A strange room that had its own odor. A newer house than the one she'd lived in. A bed, a dresser, a chair. Nothing fancy. It was a man's house.

She'd be sharing the bathroom with him. Using his shower. He'd be sleeping in another room upstairs. Her heart tightened into a little ball. Her situation had gone from bad to worse. And there was nothing she could do about it, if she stayed in Portland. She needed these people. Especially Rafe.

"I'll be right back." Rafe disappeared into the room next to the bathroom.

When she was in her own house, it felt different. Smelled different. Everything was hers. Now, everything was his.

She was too tired to think about it tonight. She'd have to trust him. She couldn't stay awake, like she did so many nights on the street, when a man had been watching her and she was afraid.

Rafe returned and handed her a T-shirt. "It isn't much but it's big and will cover you. The bed has a down comforter on it, so you'll be warm enough."

She took the shirt from his outstretched hand. "Thank you." She held it close and Rafe's clean male scent teased her nose, even though she was sure the shirt had been washed.

"Look, I'm real sorry. I did a lousy job of taking care of you tonight. I should have gotten us out of your house sooner."

"You saved my life." As she said the words she felt them deep down. Without this man, she wouldn't be alive right now. Wouldn't be sleeping in the bed in his house.

They stood in the center of the room, staring at each other. She let herself look him straight in the eye, not flinching. Or turning away. What she saw there startled her. He cared. He was sorry.

A long moment passed. His eyes were a medium brown. She hadn't noticed that before. And he was truly handsome. But he still had the power to scare her.

She was the first to turn away.

"Good night." His words were almost a whisper. He shut the door behind him.

Something had happened. She didn't know what it meant. Something passed between them. She'd made a connection with another human being.

She was beginning to like Rafe Campbell far too much.

CHAPTER 16

*R*afe opened the oven and slid in the sausage and spinach frittata. It would warm easily if Sabrina slept late. He poured a cup of coffee and sat at the table by the window. At least in his own kitchen he had more room and his favorite pots and pans to cook what he wanted.

But he couldn't stop thinking of Sabrina upstairs, in the spare bed, wearing his T-shirt. Or thinking about her coming downstairs at her house wearing only a nightshirt. His body tightened.

His cell phone rang, and the image vanished. Doug. He picked the phone up quickly and answered.

"How is she? Did she settle down last night and go to sleep?"

"She was okay when she went to bed. Still in shock, I'd say." He took a sip of coffee. "She hasn't come down yet."

"Reality will hit today. Stick close to her. She may still try to run, even without her backpack." Doug didn't sound too hopeful.

"She's scared, of course. But she still has her shop and the ability to make more money. She has more options with us than going it alone against Nathan."

"That's right. Stay positive. You're not going to fail Sabrina."

"Is that a prediction or an order?" The tone of Doug's voice had sounded more like an ultimatum.

"Don't let your past control you. Sometimes we don't have anything to say about the circumstances we find ourselves in."

"But people still die. And we can't help them."

"We're going to protect her. You're going to protect her." This was vintage Doug. The decisive voice. The warrior tone.

"I was in that living room with her when that fire bomb came through the window and exploded on the couch. Had it hit her, I couldn't have saved her." A shudder rushed through him. "She'd just walked away from the couch. We were all damn lucky."

"I won't argue with that."

Somehow he'd keep Sabrina safe from Nathan. Her life depended on him. And his life depended on him keeping her safe. He'd figured that out these past few days. She was his salvation. The curse of failure couldn't happen again. This time he'd succeed and save the woman in danger.

A woman he was attracted to when he shouldn't be. "Did you hear back from the police? Have they any leads on where Nathan is hiding?"

"Nick is on it. He called me to check on Sabrina and you, to make sure all was secure for now."

"We're fine until Nathan figures out where she is."

"Yeah. I told Alison to go along on the shopping trip this morning. Then she has to take on another case that just came up. Too much money involved to pass up."

"That's okay. If Nathan isn't driving, he's not going to be able to follow us."

"True. But today Alison can go into the fitting room with Sabrina. You can't do that. You'll watch from an outside vantage point."

"Good idea. I hadn't thought about her trying stuff on. I'm curious, if she'll buy something different or insist on the same style of clothing she's been wearing."

Doug laughed. "Her armor. You figured that out."

"Of course. She doesn't want to be touched. I've had to be very careful." Except after the fire. She'd let him hold her. His body remembered and tightened.

"Continue to be very careful." A decisive tone.

Another ultimatum?

"I will. I don't want to spook her into running. If I do anything to make her nervous, that's a distinct possibility."

"Take that as a warning."

"Are you worried I might get overly involved with her?" Might as well get all the cards on the table.

"Not really."

"Believe me, she has a thing about big men. I won't be getting close."

"See that you don't." No question this time. An ultimatum. Doug was worried about him getting emotionally involved with Sabrina. Funny thing. He wanted to. Fat chance in hell she'd let him get close.

THE CARPETED STAIRCASE cushioned and muffled Sabrina's hesitant steps. Not that she was trying to be quiet going downstairs. Rafe wouldn't yell at her like Granny did if she was startled.

She wasn't ready to face Rafe, to face anybody after her almost sleepless night.

Hunger won out as the smell of breakfast cooking drew her down the stairs.

Yet her whole body was a coiled spring, tight and unrelenting. Like the feeling she'd had riding that bus to Seattle, after her baby girl had been stolen from her. Coiled tight, yet empty.

This time her backpack had burned. Her security. That spring coiled even tighter.

The rest of her things didn't matter. What mattered was being in Rafe's house. It was different when he was in her house, protecting her. Now the house belonged to him. His territory.

"There you are." Rafe stuck his head out the kitchen door, a welcoming smile lighting up his face. How could he be so cheerful after the night they'd been through?

"I smelled something good and I'm hungry."

"Breakfast is almost ready." He darted back into the kitchen.

She stepped off the bottom stair. Rafe's house looked even larger than it had last night in the dark. Especially with sunlight bouncing off the glass-covered outdoorsy prints on the wall. A sunny April day that didn't match her mood.

She rubbed her tired eyes and went to the kitchen. Rafe was standing at the stove, wearing blue jeans and a flannel shirt, with an apron tied round his waist. Then she saw why. He used it to wipe his hands. She kept learning interesting things about him.

She sat at the table, to keep out of his way. "Something in the oven smells good."

He pulled a skillet from the oven and dished up a serving of some kind of egg dish for each of them. Toast popped up in the toaster.

He put place mats in front of her and across the table from her. "I love the smell of breakfast. My favorite meal, after a good hamburger, of course." He put a cup of coffee in front of her.

Small talk. To put her at ease. He was good at that.

Her curiosity niggled at her. "You were talking to someone earlier."

"Doug called." He set a plate in front of her, along with silverware. "Nick had called him, wanting to make sure we were all right."

"But Nathan wasn't caught." A statement. Not a question.

"No. Not yet." Her little sliver of hope skittered away.

Rafe joined her at the table, a bigger table and nicer than the one in her tiny kitchen. Six people could sit around the polished surface. From his place across from her, he had a view of the side street. He glanced out and seemed to be scanning the street before turning back and picking up his fork.

She took a bite of the egg dish in front of her. "This is delicious."

"Have you ever had a frittata before?"

"No." She took another bite, then another. She finished about half her breakfast, and set down her fork. That coil of tightness inside her tightened even further.

She blurted out the words. "This is Friday. I have to go to my shop and get things ready for Saturday, my busiest day." She had work to do. She hated that everyone else was telling her what to do and when to do it.

"We can go by the shop and see if everything is all right."

She ignored him. "I need to go by the bank to order more checks and a replacement credit card. Then I need to work on more orders." She put as much authority as she could into her words, given the circumstances. "I have several projects to finish making. I have customers waiting."

"Doug and I didn't discuss you going back to work."

"But I have to make more money. My savings are gone." She was pleading with him.

"Maybe you'll trust a bank now." A hint of sarcasm slipped into his words.

"Maybe." She drew out the single word.

"That didn't sound very positive."

"I can't change the way I live. It's my life. It's my work." And she felt it swirling away from her. Out of control.

"Finish your breakfast, before it gets cold. Then we'll talk." He was almost finished.

She stared at the food remaining on her plate. Not eating it would gain her nothing. Not with Rafe. She picked up her fork.

The doorbell rang. Her heart jumped into her throat.

"That must be Alison. Doug said she'd be coming this morning." He bolted from the chair and headed for the front door.

Another complication. She didn't need all these people. She needed to get back to work. Her independence and her livelihood were slipping away from her.

"Good morning, Sabrina." Alison greeted her with a smile.

"Uh, good morning." She didn't know how to act around these people. They were friendly and helpful and made her feel like a fraud. Like she couldn't take care of herself. Yet she'd taken care of herself since she was fifteen.

"How are you feeling today?"

"Okay." She wasn't about to admit anything else to Alison. She might be a detective, but she was a woman, and pretty. Beside her, Sabrina felt plain.

"How about shopping for new clothes to brighten your spirits?"

Oh, no. Not at all what she wanted to do. "I didn't lose much. I didn't have much. I buy my clothes at the resale outlet down the street from my shop."

Alison raised a brow.

"I hate to shop. I never waste money on clothes I don't need." Now she was being petulant. On purpose.

"You sound like Kara. You two make a pair. Clothes don't matter, but jewelry does." Alison laughed at her own meager attempt at a joke.

Sabrina touched the dangling amethyst earring in her right ear. She was wearing her favorite pair. The ones she'd worn yesterday and still had on last night. One possession she didn't lose in the fire. She'd wear them as a token. And get others from her displays that hadn't sold. She loved wearing the earrings she made. And the necklaces too.

Rafe had retreated to the sink to wash the skillet he had used and wasn't joining in the conversation.

Sabrina took her plate to the sink.

Rafe looked at her with those soft brown eyes that appeared apologetic. "We can get you some clothes first, since Alison is free this morning. She goes to court this afternoon. Then I'll take you to the bank and the shop and stay with you the rest of the day."

She studied his expression. A compromise. The best she could hope for. "I'll go get ready." She left the kitchen and headed for the stairs. She'd get a few clothes from the resale shop then go work on her orders for customers. But she wouldn't have any time away from Rafe. And his penetrating stare that sent waves of unease coursing through her.

CHAPTER 17

*R*afe scanned the area around the shop while Sabrina unlocked the front door. No one in a hooded sweat-shirt. No one lingering in the neighborhood. No immediate threats. He followed her inside and shut the door.

Doug had ordered the locks changed on the shop that morning and strong dead bolts added to both doors. The window was reinforced and a strong latch attached. The new keys were delivered to Rafe's house and were waiting for them when they returned with two bags of clothes Sabrina had reluc-tantly bought.

Used clothes. Not new. She'd refused to go to a department store and buy clothes off the rack no one had worn before. At his house, she'd changed into one of the new outfits, a blue patterned skirt, a blouse, and a light blue sweater. Still her usual armor.

Sabrina prowled the shop, front and back. "Nothing out of place." She opened the refrigerator. "Nothing has been moved from where I put it yesterday."

She glanced at him. Her open-eyed expression surprised him. She'd begun looking at him directly, at least part of the time. With those soft green eyes that had seen so much.

"Nathan must have thought the fire took care of me. I don't think he was here last night."

"He was wrong. We were ready. We escaped."

She released a big sigh. "He'll probably try again, when he figures out I'm not dead." Her statement so matter-of-fact. Like she was getting used to being targeted and surviving.

"I'll check the video. We're not taking chances."

He pulled four bottles of water out of the sack he set on the work table. Then opened the refrigerator and pushed everything to the back. He put the new bottles right in front. "Don't drink anything but these water bottles. We're taking no chances. Sodium fluoroacetate kills within six hours. It only takes a very small amount."

"I remember." She frowned and looked away. A gesture he'd come to recognize as her frustration indicator.

"Nathan can't get in easily now. The new locks and the latch on the window may keep him out."

"Good. I don't want him in here. I don't want him touching my things."

"But Nathan is cunning and lethal. We either go out for lunch or bring food with us each day. And our water."

She gave him that frown and frustrated look again. She didn't like being told what to do. Yet it was for her own safety.

She took off the sweater she'd worn over her new skirt and blouse, and hung it on the back of her chair behind the work table. Doug had turned on the heat earlier and the shop was warm and cozy. She settled into the chair and pulled two trays of beads toward her.

"I need to make some new things with the patterns I

remember. All my designs were stored in the computer. Erik put them in a cloud storage, but I don't have a computer to see them."

"You can use mine after I look at the video." He opened the cabinet and set the laptop on the table across from her. "This won't take long, if he didn't trigger the cameras."

She bit her lip. "I hope I remember how Erik told me to find the design file."

"We can always get Erik back here to help you again."

Her eyes brightened. She opened a plastic box and took out a wire and reached for her tray of red stones.

"Can you do that? From memory?" He sat in the chair across from her.

"Of course. I've made some of these designs for years. Nathan may have destroyed my laptop, but he hasn't erased my brain."

"That's the spirit."

"He's not going to defeat me. I'm going to win."

"I know you will. And we'll help."

He checked the video feed. "Nothing. He hasn't been here since Sunday night."

"Good." A timid smile from her, then she ducked her head and picked up another bead.

The bell out front rang. "Are you in the back?" It was Doug.

Rafe got up and went to the front. "We haven't been here long."

"Shopping done?" Doug raised a brow, asking a question with his eyes.

"A start. She doesn't want much. And it all had to be from the resale shop, except underwear."

"That's what Alison said when she called me. But Alison also watched what sizes she picked out and will do more shopping on her own. Sabrina will have everything she needs." His voice was quiet but emphatic.

Doug usually got what he wanted. He wanted to buy things for Sabrina. But she'd been on her own for years and was proud of her ability to take care of herself. He understood both sides of the argument.

Nathan was more than she could handle though. With Nathan, she needed help. But was getting far more help than she was comfortable with.

Doug limped into the back room and Rafe followed.

She looked up from the necklace she was making. "Thanks for the clothes. I really do appreciate all you've done for me, though I guess at times you can't tell." She managed a weak smile.

Doug and Rafe pulled out chairs and sat across the table from Sabrina.

"You're welcome. I wish I could do more, like find that damn Nathan. Excuse my language."

"I know you're trying. I appreciate it." She ducked her head back to her work, adding small gold beads to the wire."

The bell on the door rang again. "That's probably Nick. He told me he'd meet me here."

Nick ducked through the doorway and joined them around the table. "Two interesting developments."

"What's going on?" Doug's commander voice.

Nick laughed. "We've got Nathan on the run. He's vacated the motel room where he'd been staying since leaving the first motel. Showing his picture to motel personnel paid off."

Rafe glanced at Sabrina. "If the police keep him on the run long enough, Sabrina will be relatively safe."

"We also know how he got away after torching the house. A city bus. The driver remembered him."

"We still don't know where the car is." Doug leaned his cane against the table.

"He had it with him when he checked into the first motel. The license number is on the registration." Nick let the frustration show in his voice.

Rafe frowned. "Has his picture been shown on TV yet?"

"Just that blurry driver's license photo." Nick shook his head. "I've been calling people in Riley and no one seems to have a better picture of him."

"He didn't like his picture taken, even as a child." Sabrina picked at the beads in front of her. "He ran from cameras."

"How old was he when you last saw him?" Nick turned to her.

"Nineteen."

Nick pulled out the copy of Nathan's driver's license photo and pushed it across the table to Sabrina. "Will you recognize him if he walks in the door? Take a look at his picture again."

"I've tried to forget him over the years." She picked up the picture. "He still has a pointed chin. Bushy eyebrows. Evil bright blue eyes."

"Evil bright blue eyes?" Rafe glanced at Nick. He was writing on his notepad.

"His whole face looked evil to me. Like a devil. Whenever he was near me, he stared. Hard." She looked up. "He was scary."

SABRINA BENT OVER HER SKETCHPAD, moved her pencil in an arc, and tried to concentrate on the lines she was drawing. Tried to concentrate on the design in her brain. Tried to concentrate on ignoring Rafe in his recliner no more than six feet from where she sat on the couch.

The tightness in her chest wouldn't go away. A whole evening alone with Rafe.

In his house.

The rest of her freedom had been destroyed, along with her house and her belongings. She was trapped.

"I'd like to go back outside to the patio." She stood and put on the fleecy sweater beside her on the couch.

"Sure." He followed her out the door, newspaper in hand.

She sat next to the small table where they'd eaten their dinner earlier. He took the chair opposite. This time no dinner plates separated them. He was closer to her than he'd been inside the house. Not a good choice. But it would be petty to go back inside now.

She understood. A bodyguard had to stay close to do his job.

"We need more light." He stood and flipped the switch on a light fixture in the shape of a hanging lantern. "No one can see anything more than silhouettes through that bamboo shade."

He indicated the shade that hung on the street side of the patio. Bushes blocked the view at the back and the other side of the lawn. He returned to the table.

She set her sketchpad between them. Rafe leaned back in his chair and opened the paper again. And ignored her. That tightness in her chest that wouldn't go away kept her from ignoring him.

He wasn't going to leave her alone. Her only escape would be to go upstairs to her bedroom. No. She wasn't a coward. She'd been in uncomfortable situations before and survived. Nathan would be caught eventually. And she'd find an apartment to rent.

"I wish you could catch Nathan." She blurted out the words, then covered her mouth with her right hand.

"Nick's working hard. He'll find him." He reached across and patted her left hand that was resting on the sketchpad. She tensed her muscles and drew her hand back.

"I'm sorry. Reflex action. I know you don't like to be touched."

"I overreacted. I'm sorry too."

"Has someone touching you always meant pain?"

She had to think about that. "Yes, or it led to pain."

"It doesn't have to be that way." His gentle brown eyes looked almost like they were pleading with her. But there was something else in his eyes too. Warmth, maybe?

Nervous tingles skated up and down her body. She kept her gaze on Rafe. He excited her in a way she'd never experienced.

"You could touch my hand." The emphasis on my. His words sounded like a dare.

A risk. Should she? She reached out, drew her hand back, then reached again. This time she let her hand rest on the top of his big hand. His skin was rough, with coarse dark hairs.

She pulled her hand back.

His smile danced in his eyes. "You did it."

She let herself smile back. It felt strange. But she didn't say anything.

Rafe made her feel things she'd never felt before. Here she was, thirty years old, barely able to hold a conversation with a man. And finding out a touch could be nice instead of scary.

But she wasn't sure she wanted to find out where touching him could lead. Not even with Rafe.

"You had a baby at an early age. That must have been a shock to you."

She hesitated before deciding to tell him more. "I let Robert touch me because he was keeping me safe from Nathan. Not for any other reason. He pushed and pushed until he got what he wanted. What all men want."

"Some men have more control than others. And more respect for women."

Sincerity shown in his eyes. Was Rafe a man who could be trusted? So far he was.

"Have you been with any other man besides the father of your baby?"

She hesitated again, then looked down at the half completed drawing on her sketchpad. She wasn't proud of what she'd done to survive. "I needed protection when I got to Portland. A guy on the street offered to keep me safe from the pimps if I stayed with him in his tent. Of course he wanted sex as a part of the bargain."

"So you've been used rather than loved and cherished."

She looked up at him. "Love? Is there any such thing?"

"Yes. I've loved twice. Wonderful women I respected."

"But you don't have anyone now?"

"No. But I've stopped running and I hope to settle down and have a family someday. With the right woman."

"Oh." That's all she could say. Could she be the right woman for a man like Rafe? No. Too much of a risk. He needed someone who wasn't shy and reserved like she was. He needed someone like Alison, so full of life and able to do so many things. Alison could probably cook too.

Then she saw something else in his eyes. Sadness. "You didn't want to lose those two women you loved." She said it as a statement. Somehow she knew, because of that sadness.

"No. They were taken from me. Debbie turned to heroin on the streets of New York and took up with the dealer who supplied her. She eventually died of an overdose. Bethany, my wife, was killed during a random act of violence, along with our unborn daughter. A man burst into a beauty salon to kill his estranged wife and killed six other women too. My Bethany was in there getting a haircut. She didn't have a chance."

Her heart constricted. "Oh. How sad." He'd had a rough life too.

"I was a cop. But I couldn't save either of them. Just as I couldn't save my mother and my sister, when I was fifteen. After Bethany died, I decided I was a failure. So I quit the New York Police Department and headed west to find something else to do."

"How did you end up working for Doug?"

"The owner of a gun shop introduced us. I was keeping up my skills at a shooting range. Doug came out and watched me shoot and was impressed with my marksmanship. We started talking and he offered me a job on the spot. That was two years ago."

"So you found where you want to be."

"Yes, I have. Have you?" His eyes also asked the question.

"Yes. I want to stay in Portland. That's why I haven't run from here yet. I would lose too much."

"Don't run. We'll get Nathan for you."

"I still have my shop. I can earn more money. And I can rent an apartment when it's safe."

"And in the meantime, you're cooped up here with me. And missing your freedom."

She ducked her head. "Yes." A soft word.

The flickering light from the lantern sent shadows across the patio. She missed her freedom. But could she go back to living alone, working alone, not seeing anyone but her customers? She gazed up at Rafe, at his intense stare. At the blatant desire in his eyes.

She'd miss Rafe.

CHAPTER 18

*R*afe drove to the shop the next morning, stifling a yawn behind his hand. He hadn't slept much. He glanced at Sabrina. She sat demurely, looking straight ahead. They both knew something happened last night out on the patio. Something important.

She glanced his way with a shy smile. Yes, something happened. Her expression told him she felt it as much as he did. Now what? She was warming to him, accepting him as a friend. Maybe more? Was he misreading her or did she care about him?

And if so, did they dare do anything about their feelings?

Doug would be angry. At least at first. When Nick and Tricia gave in to their feelings, he was upset at first but realized they belonged together. Did Sabrina belong with him? Could he give her the love and family that she needed, whether she realized it or not?

So many questions and no answers.

But first Nathan had to be captured and prosecuted. No

crossing the line until then. He could handle the wait. He'd show her he had restraint.

He parked in the back, in the alley, and they went inside through the back door.

His arm brushed her shoulder when she passed by him and she smiled, and didn't jump away. Yeah. He needed to keep his hands off her, but he wanted to wrap his arms around her and hold her. To feel her body against his. Like after the fire.

Restraint.

Sabrina waited on a customer who had been standing outside when she opened the front door. Then they both returned to the back room. And took their usual places at the table, him at the front, her at the back by her trays of beads and gems. She settled into a rhythm he'd begun to recognize. She knew which wire, which bead, which tool to pick up. Occasionally she'd look up at him with that shy smile.

He checked the video feeds, even though the doors and window hadn't been disturbed.

Nothing recorded.

He glanced at Sabrina and his train of thought shifted. No turning back now. But he'd have to take care he didn't hurt her.

The bell on the front door rang. "I'll check first." He got up and looked into the front of the shop.

Kara held a backpack in her hands. "My first assignment since getting back last night. Doug sent this over for Sabrina. It has a new laptop in it."

"Thanks for delivering it. I hope she accepts it in the spirit in which it was given."

"What do you mean?"

"She's very independent and wants to be able to take care of herself. And now she can't and she doesn't like it."

"You seem to know a lot about her state of mind." Kara kept her voice low and she gazed at him with a questioning look.

"We've been together a lot these past two weeks." He knew it was a lame excuse.

"That's what I've heard. I also heard how you look at her. From Alison. Don't get any ideas." Her voice held a note of censure.

"I'm not doing anything to hurt her. She's a grown woman."

Kara shook her dark red hair away from her eyes. "And inexperienced. Doug's rules are to protect the client."

"I'll tell Doug if anything develops." He tried for a sincere tone. They were talking in generalities, but the subtle meaning was there too. Hands off.

Maybe.

"I'll make my delivery and be on my way." She frowned at him, then headed for the back room.

Rafe followed. Sabrina was bent over her work table, stringing blue stones on a double wire, making a bracelet. He marveled at her concentration.

"Hi, Sabrina." Kara pushed the backpack across the table toward Sabrina. "Doug sent this for you."

Her wide-eyed look said she was surprised. "I was going to buy another one this week." There was a note of displeasure in her tone.

"Doug believes we didn't do enough to protect you so the agency is replacing at least a few of the things you lost. There's a new computer inside." Kara pulled up a chair and sat.

Sabrina unfastened the latch and peered inside. Then raised her head. "That's exactly the kind I had."

"Doug asked Erik. He saw what you'd been using when he helped you with your files."

"Uh, thanks. Thanks for bringing it over." She was clearly at a loss for words. Then she brightened. "You're back from San Francisco."

"Last night. Crazy case. But now I'm here to help any way I can."

Sabrina pulled the computer out of the backpack and set it on the table.

"Erik will come by later. He'll help you get your files from the cloud and get everything working."

Rafe was sure no one had ever given her something this nice before. "I wish we could replace all the drawings you lost in your sketchpads."

"At least I have my business files. And the designs that were finished. I kept my drawings with my computer. Erik wanted to take them and scan them. I told him no. It was my fault I lost them."

"When you decide which drawings you want to save, Erik can scan them quickly. I'll take you to the agency and you can watch him do it. Then you won't lose anything again."

Kara moved toward the door. "Speaking of the agency, I'd better get back. Report to write."

"Thanks for bringing these." Sabrina indicated with her hand both the backpack and the computer.

"You're welcome." Kara headed out the front door, setting off the bell again.

"Why is everyone being so nice to me?" Sabrina said the words through gritted teeth. "I don't understand. I feel smothered. There's always someone around. I'm never alone."

Her sudden turn about startled him. "For your own safety. We don't intend to let Nathan get close."

She glanced at the backpack and computer. "If I leave now, he can't get me. He won't know where I've gone."

Her words and tone kicked him in the stomach. Maybe she

wasn't as stable mentally and emotionally as he'd thought she was. Did he really want to take on someone with problems like hers? Hell, he had his own problems. He was still digging himself out from under that dark cloud that had descended when Bethany was killed. Sabrina had lived a hard life. She might not want to settle down and live what he considered to be a normal life. Maybe it wasn't meant to be.

~

ONCE INSIDE RAFE'S HOUSE, Sabrina escaped upstairs to her room. She was caught in a web. These people were smothering her. That's what she'd said in the shop, and that's exactly how she felt.

She threw the backpack on the bed, then gasped. She opened the fastener and checked the laptop. It was okay. She hadn't hurt it.

She took off her jacket and opened the closet door to hang it up. And gasped again. More clothes hung in the closet than were there when she left for the shop. She flipped through the garments. Brand new skirts, sweaters, and long-sleeved blouses in the browns, blues, and other muted colors she liked. At one side of the closet three light-weight tops, a pair of jeans, and another pair of pants were hanging. Clothes she'd never wear. Was it Alison? Why would she buy them?

She sank to the floor. Her nerves a jumbled mess. She rocked back and forth. Her life had spiraled out of control. First Nathan, then Doug and his agency, and Rafe.

Rafe.

He was the one she feared the most. He was the one making her lose control. He was the one who scared the hell out of her.

She felt things for him she'd never felt before.

A knock on the door startled her and she jumped.

"Are you all right?"

Rafe.

Checking on her.

"Come in." She slowly rose from the floor and faced him. "Look at what someone did." She pointed at the open closet.

"More clothes. Alison figured you needed more than you'd bought. She brought them over today."

"I didn't need any more, especially those pants." Her tone sounded petulant, even to herself. "I've never had this much clothes."

"The pants and those lighter weight tops are in case you want to take a risk. Shed your armor."

"Armor?"

"The baggy clothes you hide under."

"I don't hide." Then a memory sneaked in. Her wearing her nightshirt, in the kitchen. Rafe sitting at the table in the dark.

She looked down at the floor. "I don't want men staring at me."

"Men like to stare at a pretty woman."

Her pretty? Did Rafe think so? Now she was really confused.

He ventured further into the room. "We're pushing things on you. We're interrupting your life and you feel uncomfortable."

"Yes." She noticed his change of subject.

"I want you to think about something. You've never had a family you could trust. Maybe you could learn to trust a bunch of strangers who want to help you. I know that's a big step for you. Trusting isn't easy when you've been betrayed so many times."

She gazed at him, at his dark, serious eyes. He meant it. He was offering the friendship of the people in the agency. The people who were doing so much for her.

She shuddered as jiggly nerves bounced around in her body. "I'll think about it. I don't know how to feel about everything that has happened."

"Take your time. Don't rush it. We'll just keep on doing as we've been doing. And wait to see if Nathan will try something else or if he's given up. He knows you have lots of help now."

"I don't have a choice, do I?"

"No. We're your best hope. Now I'm going to go down to the kitchen and fix dinner. Come down when you're ready."

"Okay." But she didn't feel okay.

He left, closing the door behind him. She turned back to the closet and looked through the clothes again. Examining the fabrics. Looking at the lovely colors. Alison knew what to buy. She felt guilty accepting the clothes, but she couldn't remember the last time she'd bought something new.

She might even get used to these pushy people.

Then there was Rafe. She liked his gentle brown eyes. For a big man he was quiet and kind. She could get too used to these people. Especially Rafe. And when it came time for her to leave and live her own life again, she'd be hurt. Especially if she let Rafe get any closer.

CHAPTER 19

*A*ny other Sunday morning Sabrina would be heading for her shop to work on orders for customers. She sank onto the couch in Rafe's living room. The welcoming softness of the leather soothed a bit of her bad mood. But reminded her she was in Rafe's house. Doing what he wanted. What she wanted was to work on the necklace for a customer. Waves of tension radiated through her.

He'd planned her Sunday. She hadn't. So she'd put on the clothes she'd worn the night of the fire. A blue and brown patterned skirt and a blue sweater. But without the matching heavier sweater over the top. It still had Rafe's blood on it, from the night of the fire.

Rafe hadn't said anything about her choice of clothes during breakfast.

How do you rebel when no one notices that's what you're doing?

She picked up the sketchpad with the design she'd been

working on the night before. And examined it with a critical eye. At least she had some time to recreate the designs she'd lost in the fire. And use them to make pieces to sell. To make more money, fast. To replace at least some of what she'd lost. To regain more of her independence.

She had to be able to take care of herself, completely.

Rafe came into the room and sat in his recliner. He picked up a newspaper and ignored her. She couldn't ignore him. Her concentration slipped away from the sketch. Rafe wasn't the kind of guy who would try to control, other than for her own good. He wanted her to stay safe. The perfect bodyguard, always watching.

All she did was complain.

But she wasn't going to admit defeat this morning and change her clothes. She'd wear this old skirt and sweater today. Tomorrow she'd decide if she was ready to wear something new that Alison had bought. They were pretty clothes, nice skirts and blouses and sweaters. Except for the pants and tight blouses. She wouldn't wear those. That was her old life. But wearing something new? That might be fun.

A knock on the front door startled her out of her thoughts. Rafe went to the door and Nick strolled in. He greeted her, then sat on the far end of the couch, giving her plenty of room.

She set her pad and pencils down.

Rafe went back to his chair but sat on the edge. "What's up?"

"I got another call from Mike Pearson, the Riley detective. He said the lawyer Pendergraf was the one who called the chief and told him not to cooperate with you."

"That explains why I didn't get a chance to say anything. Chief Howard challenged me as soon as I sat down."

Nick shifted on the couch. "Pearson got me the information

on the sodium fluoroacetate. The feed store owner is a long-time friend of his. Nothing missing. No tampering."

"I thought you had that information." Rafe looked puzzled.

"The owner wouldn't talk to me about it on the phone. Too suspicious."

"Did you get a list of the people who've recently bought the poison?"

"He's sending that to me today."

"This could be our big break." Rafe sounded hopeful, which raised Sabrina's hopes.

Nick stood. "Time to go. I'm on my way to pick up Tricia. We're meeting Doug for brunch. I'll be in touch."

"With answers, I hope," Rafe said. "I'm taking Sabrina to the agency this afternoon. Erik is going to meet us and scan her designs and upload to the cloud storage, with the rest of her files."

"Good idea, just in case." Nick went out the front door.

Sabrina picked up her sketchpad, but she couldn't stop thinking about Nick and Tricia. He'd come into her shop several times with Tricia and they seemed very happy together.

"Nick and Doug are really friends, aren't they?" She blurted out the words.

"Tricia is Doug's niece. Did I tell you that?"

"No. You didn't."

"Nick shot the serial killer who was after Tricia. He was her temporary bodyguard, but became much more. And moved back to Portland from Los Angeles, to marry her and join the police force here."

"Oh." Could she be more than someone Rafe was protecting? Shivers cascaded through her body. She blocked the possibility from her mind.

~

SABRINA BRUSHED a tear from her cheek and turned away from the TV. The sappy movie she'd been watching with Rafe had ended. A family reunited after a war. She glanced at Rafe, at the glistening in his eyes. She'd never known a sensitive man.

She picked up her sketchpad from beside her on the couch. To keep her hands occupied. "Do you think Doug will find my Gracie for me? She's my only family now. Granny's mind is gone. And I don't claim Nathan as family."

Rafe shifted in his recliner, adjusting the foot rest. "Gracie. That's what you called her?"

"Yes. My little Gracie. I miss her still." The void in her heart wouldn't go away. Tears threatened again, but she willed them to stop.

"Of course you do. If she can be found, Doug will find her. He's that good."

She smiled. "Everyone in the agency has been so friendly. And there are family connections too."

"Yeah. It's hard to understand sometimes, how some families can be so dysfunctional and others are normal and happy." He frowned, and she remembered his father had tried to kill him. After he'd killed his mother and sister.

"I've never been around a happy family."

"You have that wistful look in your eyes," Rafe said. "Do you wish sometimes that you were part of a nice family where people get along?"

"That won't happen. I'm taking care of myself. And Gracie if I get her back. I have to be ready to go if times get tough. If Nathan isn't caught."

"What if you find a man you can trust and you settle down and have more children?"

She shook her head. "No one is going to love me."

"You think you're unlovable?" Questioning words and a questioning gaze.

"Aren't I? My mother left me. My Granny and my cousin didn't like me. Nathan actually hated me and told me he would kill me someday."

Rafe laughed. A funny little laugh. Then he shook his head from side to side. "You are definitely lovable. All the gang in the agency would give anything to take care of you and get Nathan for you. You've made a lot of friends in the couple of weeks we've known you."

"You're just saying that." But how she wished it were true.

"No. I mean it. I'm going to say something else that I may regret. But I need to say it. You're not just a client to me anymore. I feel things for you I shouldn't."

She stared at him and her heart beat sped up. "You can't mean that."

"I sure don't want anything to happen to you. I want to protect you. I want to take care of you. I want to keep you with me."

"You're confusing me."

"I thought you were interested in me too. I've seen the way you look at me."

"Like I don't really believe you can be real. A big man who's gentle and kind."

"And I haven't taken advantage of you, have I?"

"No."

"And I won't. I'll keep my distance."

"I may not want you to keep your distance." She said the words quietly, then wondered where they had come from.

"What do you mean?"

"I've never had a kiss that wasn't unpleasant. Demanding. Or even cruel. Never a gentle kiss." She raised her eyes to his soft brown eyes that intrigued her so much.

"You sure do know how to tie a guy in knots."

She frowned at that statement. "What do you mean?"

"I've wanted to kiss you for days. But I haven't dared. I don't want to scare you or make you afraid of me."

"I'd like a gentle kiss, to see how it feels." She kept her gaze on his.

Rafe hesitated and she was afraid she'd said too much. Then he rose from his chair and crossed to the couch. He was so tall and big. He sat down next to her, his weight causing her thigh to slide toward his. When his thigh touched hers, she didn't flinch. It felt good to be this close. A shiver went up her spine, a delicious shiver.

"Okay so far?"

"Yes." And she truly meant it.

He put his arm around her shoulders and drew her close until she was against his chest. Then he tilted her chin with his hand and brought his mouth gently to hers. So feathery gentle that the flutters traveled all through her body and down to her toes. She'd never been kissed like that, so that it felt good. She shuddered and he released her.

"Still okay?"

"More than okay. That felt good."

He laughed softly. "I'm glad. That means you're making progress. You're beginning to trust."

"I guess I do trust you. I know you're not going to hurt me. You're gentle and kind."

"And you're making me feel things I haven't felt in years. I guess I'd better keep my distance or we might go over the line."

"Oh."

"Yeah. Oh."

Her insides melted into a warm glow. He'd stirred up things inside her too. And she wasn't sure about that kind of feelings.

He got up and went back to his chair. Relief cascaded through her. Now she was more confused than ever.

CHAPTER 20

The call from Nick had come while they were eating breakfast on Monday morning. They had left their dishes in the sink and headed for the shop.

Sabrina's heart pounded in her chest, beating against her ribs. The rate accelerated as they got closer. Nathan had used a crowbar to break in during the night and to destroy what he could. The question was how much damage would they find?

Rafe parked on the side street and they hurried to the back door. It stood open, the door jamb smashed. Huge gashes marred the door itself.

Sabrina's heart clenched tighter. Could it be worse than she expected? Those were angry gashes.

Rafe ushered her through the back door, gently touching her shoulder. Was that touch meant as comfort, or a hint to be strong?

Her eyes focused first on her work table. Piled high with her gems, beads, and other supplies, some spilled onto the floor. He'd used the crowbar to smash all her bins and trays. Nothing was left of them but shards of plastic. She closed her eyes, blinking back the tears, refusing to cry. He'd even smashed the chairs. What could she do now? She didn't have the money to buy new fixtures and supplies.

Nick came through the door from the front.

"I'm sorry, Sabrina. So sorry." He drew her into his arms, in a big hug. And she let him. Felt the comfort without fear. Then he released her as if realizing she might not like a hug from him.

"Not your fault. I knew he's a monster." Her voice was shaky even to her ears. "He was a monster when he was young. He destroyed every doll I ever had."

"We should have caught him by now."

Rafe's gaze shifted to the cupboard where the laptop had been. She looked too. Smashed open. No laptop.

"Was there anything else on the laptop besides the videos?" She said it quietly, hopefully.

"No, thank goodness. And it was a cheap laptop. Not too much lost. I suppose the cameras are smashed too." They both glanced up. Yes, smashed.

Nick kicked a piece of a chair out of his way. "At least you sent me copies of the videos. We still have the evidence from his previous break-ins."

Rafe went to the door into the front display area. "Holy shit. Nothing untouched here either. A crowbar does a lot of damage."

Sabrina peeked through the door, then went further into the room. Her body numb.

Nick followed them. "The fingerprint expert got some prints off the crowbar he left on the floor. We can hope they are his." His words were angry, but also resigned. "Go ahead and salvage what you can."

"Will you be able to prove it was him? If there are prints?"

"If his prints are in the databases," Nick said. "Otherwise we have to catch him first. If I can find the store where he bought the crowbar, there may be surveillance videos. I'm going to check the hardware store east of here." He went out the front door.

Sabrina stood in the middle of the front area. She didn't know where to start. Maybe with the jewelry he'd ripped from the displays and from the display cases he'd crushed and mangled. She grabbed a handful of the plastic bags under the counter and bent to pick up the necklaces, earrings, and bracelets he'd kicked around. Some were smashed enough that the individual beads and gems were loose on the floor. She picked up everything, every single bead. Each had value for her business.

Rafe bent to help her. "Go ahead and work on the pile on your table. I'll salvage what I can out here."

"Thanks." She retreated to the back room. And let the tears flow. She couldn't hold them back any longer. Her business was destroyed. The business that paid her bills. She wiped at her eyes, then scooped gems and beads into a plastic bag. As quickly as she could.

The bell from the front door tinkled. Rafe must have picked it up from the floor and rehung it. No customers would be coming through that door for a long time. She'd need new display cases and other fixtures. The only thing intact was the work table in front of her.

She wiped at her tears again and picked up another handful of beads and gems, starting a second bag. No time to separate them now. That would take hours. She had to get out of here with as much as she could. And then plan how to rebuild her business. After Nathan wasn't around to destroy it.

She'd sort everything after she bought new trays and bins to keep them in. Her heart sank. She had no money for containers.

Rafe came into the back room and set down two sacks of jewelry. "This is everything from the floor and the display cases."

"Did he take the money from the cash drawer?" She held her breath.

"Yes. I'm sorry. He didn't leave you anything but a mess."

"I'm still alive. Things can be replaced." She said the words with more bravado than she felt. She bent again to her task scooping up her supplies.

And stopped. Her sketches were under the pile. A piece of her sketchbook stuck out. She brushed at the gems and pulled the pad from under the pile. A big red X stared back at her. She paged through the pad. Every single page had a red X. He still intended to kill her.

SABRINA'S wide-eyed stricken expression ripped into Rafe's heart. More tears spilled down her cheeks. He reached for her and folded her into his arms, engulfing her with his body, molding her curves to his. He rocked back and forth, murmuring soothing sounds. And let her cry. Words were not enough.

Rafe caught movement in the doorway. Doug. His scowl was dark and deep and thunderous.

He pulled away from Sabrina. She opened her eyes and saw Doug. And shrunk into herself.

Rafe picked up the sketchpad with the red Xs and handed it to Doug.

Doug's gaze went first to Sabrina's face, then to Rafe's. His scowl remained in place.

"I need to leave. Now. He still wants to kill me." Sabrina's voice held sheer panic.

"He'd find you again," Rafe said.

"Not if I stay on the streets of a big city."

"No." Doug's voice raised to a shout. "You can't leave now. I found your daughter. You can't have her if you're on the streets."

"My Gracie? Where is she?" She stammered out the words through more tears.

"In a small town in Nebraska." Doug leaned against the wall, supporting himself with the wall and his cane. "She's with a foster family. Her adopted parents both died and she's lived in several foster homes."

"I can have her back?"

The judge in the county could award you custody."

"Will he?"

"Sounds like it. The FBI has proof she was stolen from you. She's fourteen, of course. A major adjustment for you. Instant parent of a teenager. Think about it."

She brushed at her tears. "I've had so many dreams of finding her. For many years. I've always wondered what she looked like. I only saw her for three days. She was so tiny and helpless."

"If you decide you want her back, we won't bring her here until we take care of Nathan. Can't give him another target. But I'll stay in contact with the people who have her and the judge in the county."

"Thank you, Doug. I do want her back. I always planned to find her someday." Her voice sounded stronger. "I'll rent another house or an apartment when I make more money."

Then her expression shifted. Soured like a lemon. "Nathan hasn't given up. He's only gotten meaner."

"And Nathan is driving his car again." Nick appeared in the doorway to the back room.

"How do you know?" Doug's tone was demanding.

"The hardware store down the street sold Nathan the crowbar late yesterday afternoon. He's on surveillance video. And his car is visible on the street outside the store."

"Why wasn't he driving it?" Rafe caught the implication behind Nick's words. "Where was it?"

"That's the interesting part. I had Chet recheck the towing company closest to where we know he stayed the first two nights. He just called. The car was towed and has been in storage since the day after he arrived in Portland. But hidden under a tarp at the back of the storage lot."

"Which means he couldn't have left if he had wanted to." Doug caught on.

"Which means someone sent him the money to get the car out of storage," Nick said. "It was a sizable amount, with a bonus for the owner because he let Nathan keep it covered with a tarp at the back of the lot."

"Did the owner suspect anything?" Doug asked.

"He ran the plates and the car wasn't listed as stolen."

"I thought the tow yards were all thoroughly checked." Doug scowled at Nick.

"They were. The bonus must have been a big one. I'm going to find out which officer didn't look under that tarp."

Rafe raised a brow. "The big question is what will Nathan do now that he has his car? We'll have to watch for a tail at all times."

"I'll have saturation patrols looking for the car," Nick said. "If he's driving around, we'll find him."

Doug looked directly at Rafe. "I'll give instructions for everyone to stay away from your house until Nathan is caught. That includes Nick and myself."

"I have enough food in the house for a week."

"I'll have Meagan take you anything you need. Nathan won't have seen her."

He turned to Sabrina. "Meagan is the agency receptionist."

"Oh, the woman who got us the plane tickets." Sabrina seemed to have perked up.

Then she frowned and looked at Rafe. "I need trays and bins to sort my supplies. But he took my money."

"Buy her what she needs." Doug's commanding tone.

"We'll stop on the way to my house."

"I'll get you a police escort. I'll arrange that now." Nick took out his phone.

Doug pushed off from the wall. "Rafe, I want to talk to you." He limped out to the front of the shop.

Rafe glanced at Sabrina, then followed Doug. He knew what Doug would say. And he had it coming.

"Can you keep your hands off her?" Doug didn't waste any words.

"That's the second time I've held her. The first was when her house was burning." Angry words, laced with guilt. He'd wanted so much more.

"Do not take advantage of her. She's distraught." Doug hurled angry words back at him.

"She needed comfort. I was comforting her." Anger roiled inside of Rafe, wanting out. He knew he was overstepping. His job could be on the line. But he didn't care. He'd give Sabrina what she needed. She was his priority now. Another vulnerable woman.

"I'm trusting you to protect her. Do your job. Nothing more."

"What if she wants more from me?" He kept his words quiet, so only Doug could hear. He was thinking of that kiss on Sunday that held so much promise.

"Do you know that?" Demanding words.

"Not for sure." A little bit of a lie. He'd seen the look in her eyes. She was interested.

"Do not take advantage of her." Doug repeated the words.

"I won't do anything to hurt Sabrina. You have my promise on that." Doug didn't want him to get emotionally involved with her. Too late.

CHAPTER 21

*S*abrina sat up in bed and gazed around the room. Rafe's guest bedroom. Precious little belonged to her.

A Tuesday morning and no shop to go to. Her shop hadn't burned, but it might as well have. Not much left after Nathan's destructive rampage. She shuddered at the depth of Nathan's anger.

She and Rafe would be alone in the house all day. She couldn't leave if she wanted to. Yet she wasn't afraid of Nathan getting to her when she was with Rafe.

She headed for the bathroom and the shower.

As she dried herself, she tallied in her head what was left. Her designs, some of her sketches, some of her supplies. She'd worked on her designs yesterday afternoon and finished another new design last night, after dinner. If she worked diligently, she had enough to restart her business. Here. At Rafe's house.

That's what she'd do today. She couldn't continue to live off the charity of Doug and Rafe. It was time to move on, as difficult as that would be. She felt things for Rafe that she shouldn't.

If she stayed with him much longer, she'd end up in his bed and pregnant. Rafe and his lifestyle weren't for her. He still frightened her at times, because of his sheer size.

Then there was Gracie to think about. A slow smile formed and her heart swelled. What would her daughter look like at fourteen?

She dressed in one of the new outfits Alison had picked out. A skirt that swirled around her calves and a blouse with a neckline a little lower than what she was used to. The skirt was a muted print with mainly greens and some light yellow, and the blouse a light green that matched a color in the skirt. She examined herself in the mirror, something she rarely did. She usually didn't care how she looked. Why now?

Rafe. That bothered her.

She went downstairs and found Rafe in the kitchen, frying pancakes on a griddle. Bacon strips fried alongside the pancakes. Her stomach rumbled.

He greeted her with a warm smile. And a look in his eyes that told her he liked how she was dressed. It shouldn't have pleased her, but it did.

He dished up their plates and set them on the kitchen table. "After breakfast I'll put leaves in the dining room table and add a pad. I checked. I have a piece of particle board in the shed out back. Not fancy but you'll have a worktable." An apologetic smile.

"Oh. That will work." Rafe was being nice again. Thinking about her needs.

While Rafe fixed the table for her, she moved the plastic bags of her salvaged supplies and the bags of new bins and trays into the dining room. And arranged them on the floor near the table.

First job, sort everything and figure out what she had to work with. Decide if she had enough supplies left to make the orders she had. That could be a problem. As soon as Nathan was caught, she'd start selling at the flea markets again. She had contact information on her computer and she could let her regular customers know what happened and how they could reach her.

When her life was no longer in danger.

RAFE SET his phone back on its charger and opened his laptop that sat on the coffee table. Nick had called. Said he had pictures of Nathan and the car and would email them. Rafe leaned back on the couch, waiting for the email. Less than a minute later it showed up.

"Sabrina."

She raised her head from her bead sorting. "What?"

"Nick sent a picture of Nathan and one of him with the car. Come here."

She approached him, her expression one of fear. Wide eyes. Down-turned mouth.

"You need to see what he looks like now." He said the words quietly. She had to see the picture, for her safety.

He opened the attachment and clicked on the first photo. She sat next to him, so close he could have leaned slightly and touched her. She shifted to the left, leaving several inches between them, and peered at the screen.

That subtle scent of hers teased his nose. And his libido. He moved so she could scoot over in front of the laptop. He wanted much more than she was ready to give. More kisses, more touches. Her in his bed.

"That's Mr. Nickerson's old car, for sure. Paint off one fender. It looks even more beat up now." She looked up at him. "Nathan never took care of anything he owned."

He clicked on the other photo. Nathan by himself. "Do you see any resemblance to Nathan as a young boy?"

"He was nineteen when I left. He looks the same. Just a bit older." She gazed at him again, then back at the photo. "That sarcastic grin of his. I'd know it anywhere. And the pointy chin we saw on the video. The slightly haughty look, even when relaxed against the car." She shuddered. "Where did the pictures come from?"

"A friend of that detective, Pearson. His daughter is Nathan's current girlfriend. She took the pictures and he borrowed them long enough to scan them for me."

"I can't imagine him with a girlfriend. He's such a creep."

"Pearson also found out this friend of his has some sodium fluoroacetate stored in a shed. He raises cattle and uses it to bait coyote kills. Nathan might have stolen the poison from him."

"He's a user. So he used the daughter to get to the poison her father had. Makes sense."

Rafe chuckled. "You'd never give him the benefit of the doubt."

"Never." She wore an indignant expression.

"Study this photo carefully. Make sure you'll recognize Nathan if you see him here in Portland."

"Oh, I'll recognize him now if he's close enough. His features are still distinctive."

"My job is to not let him get that close." Frustration rode his voice.

She looked up at him again. Held his gaze. Her eyes telling

him she was feeling that attraction simmering between them. She bounced up, then retreated to her worktable and more sorting.

Rafe watched her for a minute, then stood and headed to the kitchen. He had to get away from her and the draw she had for him. As if small wires were attached between them, pulling him toward her.

It was too early in the afternoon to start dinner. Cookies. Baking cookies would get his mind off Sabrina.

When he took the first pan from the oven, Sabrina appeared at the kitchen door.

"Something smells delicious in here." She stayed in the doorway.

Rafe put the second pan into the oven and used a spatula to move the still hot cookies to a plate to cool. He put the plate on the table. "I don't know about you, but I love cookies right out of the oven."

"I've never had them that way. We ate store bought cookies."

"Your granny didn't bake?"

"A waste of money, she always said. And she wouldn't let me learn to bake either."

"I'm not liking your granny very much."

She looked down at the floor. "I didn't always like her much either."

Rafe resisted the urge to pull her into his arms and comfort her. "Sit down. Do you like milk with your cookies?"

"It's been many years since I've had milk and cookies."

Warm and fuzzy feelings welled up inside of him. He'd found a way to please her.

They sat at the table, a plate of cookies between them and each with a full glass of cold milk. "You're spoiling me." She wiped at her milk mustache with a napkin. "I'm never going to want to leave."

"Maybe that's what I'm aiming for." A dangerous thought, but it was the truth. "I like having you around. I like doing things for you."

She took another bite of cookie and a dab of chocolate clung to her lip. Her gaze met his. Then she looked away, a blush reaching her cheeks.

"I didn't mean to upset you." He hadn't thought about her reaction. "I was joking more than anything. But I do like having you around."

"But you're always having to take care of me. I'm not taking care of myself." Fear flashed in her eyes.

"It's part of my job description as a bodyguard. You got burned out of your house. I have a house with plenty of room. So I brought you here."

"I feel guilty. You and Doug and the other people who work for him have done too much for me already."

"You have no reason to feel guilty. It's not your fault the police haven't caught Nathan. And I know they're trying hard to find him."

"I'm safer than I was. By myself. But my independence is gone. I've lost so much."

"I'm truly sorry we haven't caught him yet. He's cunning and resourceful." Rafe's stomach knotted. He hadn't done his job. He was failing another woman. And now she was completely dependent on him.

She was in his house. And he wanted her in his bed. He'd be fighting that temptation the entire time she was here. They had to find Nathan soon. Before anything happened he'd regret later. Or she'd regret.

CHAPTER 22

*A*fter breakfast the next morning that included another chocolate chip cookie, Sabrina headed for her improvised work table in the dining room. Away from Rafe. He was a distraction she didn't need if she was going to rebuild her business.

She did a quick inventory of the supplies she had left. And picked up her small stack of orders, thumbing through them.

A sinking feeling settled into her stomach. She'd need more supplies to finish all the pieces she had orders for. Nathan had destroyed too much.

Would she ever be independent and alone again?

She took a deep breath and picked up the necklace she'd started the day before. The next item she'd promised to one of her best customers. At least she had enough to finish this one.

She pulled the tray of blue gems and beads closer, and picked up a medium size blue sodalite, then strung it on the wire. She loved the dark blue color and loved the simplicity of her new design.

She glanced out the window to her left, wondering how to get the finished necklace to the woman. Wondering when Nathan would be caught. Wondering when she'd get her life and business back to the way it was.

Never back the way it was. Her house was gone. Her savings were gone. Her shop virtually destroyed.

Rafe wandered into the dining room with a cup of coffee. "Are you ready for a refill?" He smiled in that sweet way of his that made her feel like a valuable person, not a throwaway.

"Oh, I can get it for myself."

He picked up her cup. "I'll get it." He headed back to the kitchen.

Her pulse picked up. Typical Rafe behavior she was getting too accustomed to.

He was her protector. Yet in the beginning she'd been afraid of him. Now she was afraid of the effect he had on her. She craved a closeness with him she'd never had with another human being.

His hand brushed hers when she reached for the cup and took it from him. A jolt of awareness ran up her arm. "Thanks." She couldn't say any more.

He looked at the necklace she was making. "Do you have what you need to keep working?"

"For a couple of days, then I'm going to need some things I can get online." She scrunched up her eyes.

"What is it?"

"I have to wait until I get my new credit card before I can order what I need."

"I'll let you use mine."

"No. You've done enough. Doug's done enough." She glared at him.

"Can you work on more sketches and designs when you use up the supplies you have?"

That sinking feeling came back. She was trapped again. "I guess I can and my customers will have to wait. I hope I don't lose business." The words sounded desperate even to her.

"We'll have to trust that Nick will catch Nathan. Once he's in jail, you can start putting your business back together." His glance was pure compassion, mixed with that male predatory look she knew so well. Yet Rafe had never stepped over the line with her, except for that one kiss she'd asked for.

With a small smile, he took his own cup of coffee into the living room and sat in his reading chair. Close yet not too close. He was such a temptation. What if she encouraged him? She'd seen that look in his eyes. He was interested. Her whole body tingled with an awareness of him as a man. She'd never felt like this before. She'd never been interested in sex, yet now she wondered how it would be with Rafe.

No. She might never see him again when Nathan was caught and jailed. He'd go on to another assignment. If she wasn't careful, she could end up in Rafe's bed. And pregnant again.

TWENTY-FOUR HOURS later Sabrina's mind set had changed completely. Twenty-four hours of heated looks, yet staying a discreet distance from Rafe. When that wasn't what she wanted.

She craved his touch. She craved a hug. She craved a kiss. A connection. Something to make her feel alive and appreciated. And not so alone.

He'd followed her out of the kitchen.

"Shall we talk about this?" He came up behind her and

grasped her shoulders, gently turning her around. She leaned into his touch. No longer afraid. No longer walking away.

"I don't want to talk. I want to feel." She closed her eyes and settled against his chest. And breathed in his pure male essence. No longer fighting against what she wanted.

With gentle pressure he raised her chin. And captured her mouth. Another gentle, fluttery kiss. Then it deepened, strengthened, drew her in until she was kissing him back.

Rafe pulled away first. "Are you sure this is what you want?" His breathing was ragged.

She opened her eyes, her own breath shallow, but rapid. Her heart hammered in her chest. "Yes. I'm not afraid. I know you won't hurt me."

He gazed at her, long and hard. Then pulled her down on the couch with him. And turned so he was half-facing her.

Her former panic had fled. Being close to him felt safe and... something else. Something quivering in her body. Nice feelings. Needy feelings.

"Please. Kiss me again." She whispered the words.

He smiled. A wondrous smile that lit up his whole face. He pulled her into his arms and held her gently. His mouth came down on hers, and he moved his lips in a way that made her whole insides tingle. Awakening nerve endings she didn't know she possessed.

She leaned closer. Wanting so much more. Her body tingled all the way down to her toes. She'd never felt like this before.

He moved back, breaking the kiss, and leaned against the couch. "You're so sweet. I feel like I'm taking advantage of you. I don't want you to feel pressured. If I do something you don't want me to do, tell me to stop. I will. That's a promise."

Did she dare? "What if I tell you not to stop?" Gentle kisses were nice. She wanted to know if sex could be nice and gentle and feel good. Not like she was being used and then tossed away.

"Okay." His eyes searched hers. "We can see where this leads."

His voice was soft yet masculine. His scent intoxicating. "I don't want to do anything that makes you uncomfortable."

Was he too much of a man for her? Would he crush her and her spirit? Somehow she didn't think so. She moved closer.

He kissed her again and she strained against him.

"Shall we go upstairs?" Another gentle kiss. A promise of more to come?

She nodded. Not trusting her voice.

He stood and pulled her up, keeping hold of her hand. They went up the stairs and into his bedroom with the king-sized bed. Her heart beat faster. But not from fear. From anticipation.

She could, if she wanted, go back downstairs to the living room. But she didn't want to.

He stopped before he reached the bed and pulled her into his arms again. For another gentle kiss.

She gazed into his brown eyes. "I've had sex many times. But it was never good for me. Just for the guy."

Another smile broke across his face. "I'll try to make it good for you. When we make love, we both should get satisfaction."

With the next kiss he let more passion show. He was aroused already. She pressed against him and he groaned. The kiss went on and on, deeper and deeper, drawing her in. She opened her lips and let him inside. His tongue tangled with hers, sending those tingling sensations careening through her body.

He carefully undressed her before stripping off his own clothes. Then he pulled back the covers on the bed and laid her gently down. And lay down beside her, kissing her and tasting her until she thought she'd burst from the frustration of wanting. He worshiped her body with his tongue and his eyes and his hands.

She started trembling and couldn't stay still. "Let yourself feel," he whispered. "Let go and let me take you somewhere you've never been."

He stopped long enough to sheath himself. No pregnancy this time. Then he entered her, slowly. "Still okay?"

"Mmm." Words wouldn't come.

A strange response built inside her. "This feels…different…"

"Let yourself feel." He whispered the words again.

He moved inside her, sparking sensations that affected her whole body. Again and again. And again. Time seemed to stand still. The sensations in her body built higher and higher until she careened to a peak, a far off place so high she'd never reached it before. When she thought she could stand no more, she shuddered her release and slid down the slope to feel him explode inside her. He grasped her tightly and rolled to the side, cradling her against his strong body.

She shivered against him. "Wow! I never knew it could like that."

He laughed. "Wow is right."

She snuggled into his warm body and closed her eyes. Now she knew what she'd been missing all those times.

But she couldn't keep doing this with Rafe. She didn't belong with a man like him. And she shouldn't have led him on. Did she make a huge mistake?

She needed her independence. She needed to get her daughter back and start a new life. Just the two of them. In another city if she had to.

~

RAFE SLAMMED THE CUPBOARD DOOR. Then winced.

What the hell? He'd made love to Sabrina and was blown away by the emotions she brought out in him. He couldn't deny his feelings any longer. He not only wanted her in his bed, he wanted her in his life, permanently.

But that wasn't going to happen.

He'd made love to a very vulnerable woman. Doug had warned him, but he hadn't heeded the warning.

She'd said last week that she didn't want a relationship. Didn't plan on more children. The big question—what does she want now?

Keeping her here at his house was a bad idea.

The alternative had been a hotel room.

She was safer here. From Nathan, but not from him.

He opened the refrigerator and put in the bowl of salad he'd made for later. Sabrina was still sleeping upstairs in his bed. She must have been exhausted from so many sleepless or disturbed nights.

He sat at the kitchen table and opened his laptop. Then logged into his email account. One from Doug. Asking if Sabrina was all right. Asking if he was concentrating on the job he was doing, protecting her.

Oh, hell. Now wasn't the time to answer. And Doug had sent the email two hours earlier.

A faint rustling in the hallway pricked at his awareness. Sabrina appeared in the kitchen door. "I fell asleep."

She smiled, a shy smile that told him she was feeling guilty going to sleep so quickly.

"No need to look guilty. You needed the sleep. It's normal to sleep when you're feeling satisfied."

She blushed and turned away. "I wanted to know what good sex felt like."

"And now?" He waited. Was that all she wanted?

"I go back to making my jewelry and creating more designs. You keep protecting me from Nathan, until he's caught." Her green eyes challenged him.

"Here I was feeling guilty that I took advantage of you." He watched her face for a reaction.

She flinched. Obviously she had plans that didn't include a man. She wouldn't be sharing his bed with him.

He took a deep breath. He'd have to back off, not expect more from her. As difficult as that would be.

RAFE'S CELL phone vibrated in his pocket. He'd stayed in the kitchen after breakfast, reading his newspaper at the table. Giving Sabrina space.

He pulled out the phone and answered. It was Doug. "Any good news for us?"

"Not good. But news," Doug said. "Pearson called Nick. Sabrina's grandmother is near death. And Nathan resurfaced in Riley and went to work this morning as if nothing had happened."

"And the police still don't have any solid evidence that he's behind the attacks on Sabrina in Portland." Rafe stated it as a fact.

"You've got that right."

"So, what do we do now?"

He went to the doorway and glanced at Sabrina. She was at the dining room table, working on the necklace she'd started last night. While he kept his distance. He returned to the kitchen table and took a sip of his coffee.

"You have a decision to make." Doug's tone was grim. "Do you take Sabrina to Riley to see her grandmother before she dies? And risk seeing Nathan too? Or do you not tell her and stay here with her?"

"You're leaving that decision to me?"

"Yes. You're the one who knows Sabrina better than any of us. You know how she feels about her grandmother. You saw her in Oklahoma and in that nursing home with her grandmother."

Rafe heaved a big sigh. "That's a tough one. My instincts say keep her here and safe. But that's not fair to Sabrina. She's been without family for so long. To lose her last remaining link, besides that rat Nathan, is a big blow to anyone."

"And you don't want to get on the bad side of Sabrina either." This time Doug's tone was almost teasing.

"There's that." He tamped back the guilt that arose. He couldn't get past the feeling that he took advantage of her. "I admire her and her courage. She'd want to go, whatever the risk."

"I was afraid you'd say that."

"You don't agree?"

"Yes, I agree. Family is important, whatever is left of it." Doug was obviously thinking of his own situation.

"Okay, I'll ask her if she wants to go."

"Ask me what?" Sabrina stood in the doorway.

"Go ahead and talk to her," Doug said. "I heard that question. Let me know what she decides."

"Okay." He ended the call and set the phone on the table. "Come here. There's some new developments."

She sat on the other side of the table, far enough away that he couldn't touch her without reaching across the table. Okay, she was keeping her distance. Like before. Yesterday afternoon wouldn't be repeated.

"Nathan has been found?"

"In a manner of speaking. He's back in Riley, at work today as if nothing has happened."

"That sneak! That's what I'd expect from him, since he couldn't find me."

"Or kill you." He had to add that, to make sure she remained cautious.

"So, what happens now?" Her wide-eyed expression displayed her fear.

"There's more. Your grandmother is close to death. Doug wants to know if you want to go back to Riley to see her."

"Oh." She thought a minute. Obviously weighing the risks. "Yes. I want to go." She said the words decisively, once she'd decided. He liked that about her.

"You'll most likely see Nathan while we're there. Can you handle that?"

She closed her eyes and took a deep breath. Then opened them. "Yes. I won't know what to say to him, but I'm not afraid to see him, as long as other people are around." This time her words weren't decisive, but hesitant. She'd be cautious.

"We'll make sure of that."

"When can we leave?"

"As soon as the arrangements are made. I'll call Doug back and he'll have Meagan book our flights and motel rooms."

"I'm scared. Nathan is cunning and sly."

"I know. We'll do what we can to keep him away from you."

"It may not be enough." She jumped up.

"Are you sure you want to risk going?"

"I have to. For Granny." She turned and fled the room.

That bleak look on Sabrina's face made his heart constrict,

aching for her. He'd protect her, with his life if he had to. She was that precious to him. He glanced at the doorway where she'd disappeared.

Had he fallen in love with shy little Sabrina?

CHAPTER 23

*R*iley wasn't as scary to Sabrina the second time they drove into the little town. The morning sun lit up the sky to the east, with stripes of gold and pink, a sight she would never tire of.

They'd flown first class, on an overnight flight, so they could sleep on the plane. At least she hadn't been shoulder to shoulder with Rafe, but guilt over the cost of the trip bothered her. She owed Doug so much.

"We'll go check into the motel and change our clothes before we go see your grandmother." Rafe turned off the highway and into the motel parking lot.

"Thanks. I guess I'm not quite ready. She's dying and I don't want her to die."

Thirty minutes later Sabrina scrunched up her nose at the medicinal smells of that long hallway. The door to her grandmother's room was closed. Not a good sign. Her heart spe
Was she already gone?

Rafe opened the door for her and she stepped inside the room. The curtain had been pulled so that Granny had privacy. Granny looked the same as she had the last time she was there. Curled up in the bed. Not moving. An IV connected her to her fluids and medication.

Sabrina walked toward the bed, slowly. She picked up Granny's hand. It was cold. She bent close to her ear. "Granny, it's Sabrina. Can you hear me?" She kept her voice low.

No visible sign.

"I'll be back in a few minutes," Rafe said. "I'm going to check on something." He closed the door when he left.

Sabrina turned back to the bed and her comatose grandmother. She looked so pale. And her breathing was ragged. Sabrina pulled a chair over, close to the bed, and sat.

Rafe returned in a few minutes. "I talked to the receptionist at the desk. Nathan was here last night and spent time in the room alone with your grandmother. It was after his visit that she started exhibiting signs of a slowing heartbeat and breathing problems."

"Could he have done something to her medications?"

"We're going to check on that. She has notified the doctor on call and he's on his way. Not your grandmother's doctor."

"Good. I don't trust him." She turned back to Granny. "I have an awful feeling that Nathan did something."

The receptionist came to the door and asked to come in. "Yes," Rafe said. "What is it?"

"I talked to the nurse's assistant who administers the medications for the patients. She told me Nathan was asking questions about the IV drip that includes her morphine."

"Questions about dosage?" Rafe asked.

"Yes."

A knock on the door. Rafe let the doctor into the room.

"I'm Evan Lindley, the doctor on call. What's the problem?"

Sabrina stood. "Doctor Lindley, I'm Mrs. Walter's grand-daughter, Sabrina Walters. My grandmother is having difficulty breathing. Could she be getting too much morphine?"

"I'll check." He picked up her chart, then looked at the control on the drip. "Someone has increased her dose. No wonder she's having difficulty breathing. She could go into respiratory failure at any time."

"Can you reverse the damage?" Rafe asked.

"Maybe. Maybe not. Who did this?" He looked around.

The receptionist stepped forward. Rafe nodded at her. "Her grandson, Nathan Prescott, was asking questions about the morphine drip. It may have been him when he was in the room alone with her last night."

The doctor grimaced. "It was not increased enough to cause instant death, but a slow death as her breathing becomes more difficult." He looked at the receptionist. "I'll have to report this to the police. They'll have to determine if it was a deliberate act to speed up her death."

Sabrina glanced at Rafe, the grim expression on his face. But he wasn't saying anything about Nathan trying to kill her too.

"Please. Decrease the dose for her." Sabrina tried to keep the begging tone out of her voice.

"I'll have to dial it back slowly. If she's been on the increased dose all night, it may be too much of a shock to her system." He fiddled with the control and then stepped back. "That may help. But it may not. She could go at any time. I'm sorry."

The receptionist left the room.

Sabrina's heart clenched. She sat in the chair next to the bed and stroked Granny's hand. *If it's your time, go ahead and go,*

Granny. I'll understand. And I do love you. She didn't say the words out loud, but felt them in her heart.

"Can you have Nathan arrested today?" Rafe asked the doctor.

"Do you have any reason to believe he wants her dead? Could it be for compassionate reasons?"

"I believe he simply wants her money," Rafe said.

"And who are you?"

"I'm a private detective and Sabrina's bodyguard, from Portland, Oregon. I accompanied her to Oklahoma because she has reason to fear Nathan."

The doctor frowned. "Contacting the police immediately won't help Mrs. Walters."

"But it might help Sabrina."

"I'll talk to the chief. But as frail as she is, I doubt there will be any charges filed."

Sabrina continued to stroke her grandmother's cold, gnarled hand. Fighting the tears behind her eyes.

"I have a couple of other patients to see. I'll come back." The doctor left the room.

"That police chief. He won't do anything to Nathan, will he?" She looked up at Rafe, at the compassion in his eyes.

"Probably not."

Then she picked up Granny's hand and held it loosely. And sat there for a long time, holding Granny's hand, thinking of what might have been if Granny had let her stay. Yet there was no anger in her heart. Not anymore.

The heart monitor started beeping.

An aide passing in the hall heard it and came in. "I'll get the doctor."

Sabrina stayed in the chair, holding Granny's hand, watching the line on the monitor.

The doctor came through the door, then reached over and turned off the machine. "Are you all right with letting your grandmother go? According to her chart, she's eighty-five years old."

"Oh, I had no idea. She never told anyone her age." Sabrina nodded. "Yes. It's her time. She's suffered enough." She stood, then bent down and kissed Granny's withered cheek. Her skin had turned ashen pale. She was slipping away.

Sabrina let her tears flow unchecked.

Rafe moved to her and enfolded her in his arms. The comforting strength of his body told her she'd be all right with him. It was that instant that she knew how much she loved Rafe Campbell, the most gentle, caring man she'd ever met.

But Nathan was still out there. Still a danger.

THEY FOUND PENDERGRAF'S OFFICE, tucked away behind another building on Main Street. As they approached the outer door, Sabrina's heart beat escalated, pounding against her ribs. Pendergraf had called an hour ago and said he'd meet with them at one o'clock. On a Saturday.

Granny's death had changed a lot of things. Someone had called Pendergraf. The doctor? The nursing home? Then he'd called her and gruffly told her he'd meet with her to discuss her grandmother's will. Like he was doing her a favor instead of acting as someone who worked for her grandmother.

Rafe pulled open the door and Sabrina went in, Rafe right behind her. Loud voices came from the rear of the building. Sabrina froze. "That's Nathan with him." She kept her voice at a whisper.

"Get out of here now." Pendergraf's tone was menacing. "I'll give you your money later. Then you're leaving town."

"No, I'm not leaving. I don't believe you. Granny had lots of money.

"Not any more. Leave now, before Sabrina gets here."

"This could get interesting." Rafe slammed the front door.

"Too late. She's here. I want to see the little bitch." His voice carried to the front.

Rafe tapped twice on the office door, then opened it.

Pendergraf stood, but stayed behind his desk. "Come in." He was still as thin as he always was. But only a fringe of gray hair remained on his head.

Sabrina's stomach knotted, a feeling familiar from her childhood. She hung back.

Rafe urged her forward, with a hand on her back. "I'm right here."

His voice and his touch gave her confidence. He pulled out a leather chair for her, then sat between her and Nathan.

She leaned around Rafe and glared at Nathan. "Why did you kill Granny? Why did you speed up her death?"

A grownup version of his childish smirk shown on his face. "I didn't do anything to the old lady. Who told you that?"

"The doctor." She didn't elaborate. She didn't have to. Fear danced in his eyes.

Pendergraf dropped into his chair, a grim expression on his face.

She pressed on. "You destroyed my house and my shop, but you didn't destroy me." She put as much venom in her words as she could, then sat back in her chair.

"Oh, she found her voice. The shy little bitch has claws." Nathan stood and bent over her, invading her space. "I didn't touch your stuff. And I didn't kill Granny."

She cringed, but met his gaze. "And you're still the lying bastard you've always been."

"You're the bastard. I knew who my father was."

Rafe rose and pushed Nathan away. "Don't touch her. Sit down. Keep your mouth shut unless spoken to." Anger oozed from his words.

"Keep your hands off me." Nathan glared at Rafe, but sat down.

"Here. Here. Settle down, all of you." Mr. Pendergraf sat in his chair. "Who are you, anyway?" He aimed his question at Rafe.

He sat. "You know who I am. Rafe Campbell. You've been talking to Chief Howard."

"Why did you come back here?" he demanded.

"Because we were told Sabrina's grandmother was close to death," Rafe said. "Sabrina wanted to see her again. She was with her grandmother when she died this morning. And so was the doctor who came to check her morphine level at the request of the nursing home."

Nathan's gaze was on Rafe. Sabrina was glad Rafe was on her side and not against her.

"You called Sabrina about the will," Rafe said. "First question, when was this will written?"

"Seven years ago," Pendergraf said. "Two years before she had that fall that put her in the nursing home."

"What fall?" Sabrina asked.

"She fell down the stairs and broke her hip." Nathan glared at her. "She had to go in the nursing home. I couldn't take care of her."

The knot in Sabrina's stomach grew larger. She could have helped Granny if she'd been here.

Rafe nodded to Mr. Pendergraf. "Go ahead and read

the will."

The lawyer cleared his throat and opened the file folder on his desk. "Let's begin." He read in a monotone voice, pausing only once to look up at the three of them. When he finished, he set down the pages.

"Sabrina and Nathan, the two of you split everything equally. As executor, I have charge of dividing what's left of her estate after the rest of the bills are paid." He looked at them over the top of wire-rimmed glasses. "I assume you both want the house to be sold."

"You still haven't told us how much money is there." Nathan said. "Granny had lots of money in that trust fund. And money in the bank. She told me she did."

"And I told you there's very little left. She was in that nursing home for five years. Getting full care."

"No way." Nathan jumped up. "The old lady told me she was rich. That I'd be rich someday too. She wouldn't give me money early. Said I had to keep working. Said I had to wait for my inheritance."

Sabrina slunk back against the chair. That knot in her stomach tightened further.

Nathan lunged across the desk and grabbed Pendergraf by the lapels on his suit. "Why'd you tell me where I could find Sabrina? You set me up. You wanted me to get rid of her. Why?"

Rafe jumped up, pulled Nathan off Pendergraf, shoved him back in his chair. Then stood over him, with a glare that dared him to move again.

Nathan glared back at Rafe, then at Pendergraf. "What did you do? Embezzle all her money? You wanted to get rid of both of us. So you wouldn't get caught."

Pendergraf stood. "You're talking crazy. Get out of here."

"I'm not going anywhere." Nathan still glared at Pendergraf.

Once Nathan settled, Rafe sat down again next to Sabrina. A cold chill ran down her spine. Pendergraf wanted her dead too.

"Who inherits if Sabrina and I are gone?" Nathan started to jump up again, but Rafe pulled him down.

"Sit."

Then he reached over and grasped her arm. Cautioning her. They knew nothing about her daughter. She needed a will now herself. She had a daughter to take care of. A shiver of delight lightened her mood.

"So, what does that leave us?" Nathan's voice took on a whining tone.

"A house that's falling down because you didn't help her maintain it." Sabrina was enjoying her newfound freedom to say what she wanted. "And anything inside that hasn't been sold or stolen."

"Are you saying I stole things from the house?"

"Yes. I noticed the silver tea set and some paintings were missing when I was in there last time I came to town. Anything you took and sold before she died was stolen. So where's the money you got?"

"Oh, no. You aren't going to get a thing if I don't. I'll sell the house next."

"We'll sell the house. It's half mine."

"You wouldn't talk so big if your boyfriend wasn't with you."

"Rafe is my bodyguard. Not my boyfriend."

That earned a wide-eyed look from Nathan. He hadn't considered that possibility.

"You had no right to sell anything belonging to Mrs. Walters, before her death," Mr. Pendergraf said. "Sabrina is right. That's burglary."

"Granny wouldn't give me any money. Then I had to put her

in that home. I sold what I could. Are you going to put me in jail for that?"

"That was your mistake." Sabrina glared at him. "Her income wasn't high enough to cover the cost of the nursing home and her savings had to be used."

"You bitch. You'll get what's coming to you." Nathan stormed out of the office, slamming the door.

CHAPTER 24

*R*afe waited until he was outside Pendergraf's office before pulling out his phone. Two messages. He'd felt the vibrations when the calls came in, but couldn't answer. Not with Nathan sitting there. And Pendergraf.

"Calls you missed?" Sabrina's tone was subdued.

"Doug and Nick. I'll call them from the motel."

They stopped at the diner to pick up coffees to go and headed for the motel.

Once inside his room, Sabrina immediately scooted through the door to her own room, closing the door.

He gazed at the door. She was keeping her distance, both physically and emotionally. He accepted it, but didn't like it.

She had turned to him in her grief, at the nursing home when Granny died. She'd wanted comfort, but that seemed to be all she wanted. At least for now. Hope lived in that thought.

Besides, he needed time too. To think. To plan. He glanced at the closed door again. She was still in danger.

He sat at the small desk, opened his laptop and turned it on.

Then sipped his coffee as he pulled out his phone. He tapped Doug's number. Doug answered immediately.

"I was worried when you didn't answer."

Was that an accusation? "We were in the lawyer's office and Nathan was there. I couldn't leave the room."

"So you did get an appointment. Okay. That's valid. What happened?" More Doug speak.

"Nathan is mad as hell. Ready to attack Pendergraf. Accuses him of setting him up by telling him where Sabrina was. To get rid of both of them. Then accused him of embezzling the money."

"Embezzling?"

"According to Pendergraf, there's very little money left. Nathan swears Granny told him she was rich and he'd be rich someday. Mrs. Murphy told us she'd inherited from her father who had made a fortune in the railroads as an executive."

"Granny?" Doug laughed.

"Yeah, well, I felt sorry for her, dying like that." He took another sip of coffee.

"I got your message that she was gone. I'm sorry."

He shifted in his chair. "Whatever she did in her younger days, she didn't deserve to die all alone in that nursing home. At least we were there with her at the end."

"That must have been a comfort to Sabrina."

"Yeah. And Pendergraf said he'd handle arrangements for a graveside service and burial, for Monday." Rafe snickered. "Appropriate, since he controls the money."

He stood and paced from the desk to the bed and back again. "But…"

"Yeah?"

"Nathan is still threatening Sabrina. His hatred runs deep.

Sabrina told me he'd been an angry child. Now he's an angry man and lashing out."

"Stay right with her. And let Nick know about Nathan accusing Pendergraf of embezzlement. Pearson should look into it."

"Nick called earlier too. I'll call him next. I'd like to meet Pearson, since we have to wait around here until after the funeral on Monday." And he and Sabrina would be together all day Sunday. Alone together, unless he could figure out some-thing to do to get them out of the motel but still keep her safe.

"Nick can arrange a meeting. Out of town would be best. We don't want the chief to know he's talking to you."

"That could work. And get us out of the motel for a while at least."

"Where is she now?"

"In her room, with the door closed between us. We come and go through the door to my room."

"Good thinking. And I'm assuming that door is closed at night." Doug's tone was unmistakable. Hands off.

"Yes." He could answer that truthfully. Though guilt soared through him. He didn't want that door between them. She did.

Rafe heard a woman's voice asking Doug a question. Where to turn? "Where are you?"

"Pulling into the motel parking lot. Alison is dropping me off, then heading out for another assignment."

What the hell. Rafe went to the door and opened it. And there was Doug, getting out of an SUV.

Alison turned off the engine and got out. "Hi, Rafe."

"Hi yourself. This is a surprise." And he wasn't sure he liked it. Doug showing up now, to supervise.

She smiled. "You ought to know your unpredictable boss by

now." She opened the back end and Rafe took Doug's suitcase for him.

"My room is the other side of Sabrina's. I'll get the key later."

"And I have my assignment." Alison got back into the SUV and with a wave, drove off.

"So, why did you come?" Rafe set Doug's suitcase inside the door, then closed the door behind Doug.

Doug limped to the chair Rafe had vacated and dropped into it, setting his cane on the floor. "Nick is arriving tomorrow morning, on a red-eye. He's getting a warrant today for Nathan Prescott's arrest."

Rafe sat on the bed. "And you didn't want to fly on the red-eye."

"There's that." He stared hard at Rafe. "And I wanted to check up on Sabrina, and you."

"I'm not going to hurt her." Truth be told, she was hurting him.

"Keep it that way."

Change of subject needed. "Why the warrant? What do you know that I don't?"

Sabrina opened the door and peeked in.

"Come on in, Sabrina. I just got here." Doug motioned to her.

"Hi...Doug. Good to see you." She looked at him expectantly. "I heard Rafe say warrant."

"Nathan wasn't wearing gloves when he bought the crowbar from the hardware store. And he missed a couple of prints that he thought he'd wiped off." Doug smiled. "And the surveillance camera in front of the hardware store picked up his car and license plate number. A surveillance camera across the street from the shop shows him, through the window, hacking at the display cases."

Rafe laughed. "Major mistakes. He got careless."

Doug joined in the laughter. "He was in a hurry to get out of town when he did the smash job on the shop."

Sabrina stood near the desk. "That means he can be arrested and sent back to Oregon?" She looked at Doug, then Rafe.

"Once he's caught," Doug said. "The bad news is he's in hiding. Not at home, according to Nick. He said Pearson is looking for Nathan now."

Rafe retrieved his phone from the desk, then sat down on the bed again. "Maybe that's what Nick was going to tell me when he left me the message to call." He tapped Nick's number.

"Tell him I'm here," Doug said.

Nick answered.

"Doug's here. Told me about the warrant."

"Good. That's why I called. And one more thing. Make him tell you the other reason he hightailed it to Oklahoma. See you tomorrow." He ended the call.

Rafe stared at the phone. Then at Doug. "Okay. What's the other reason you're here?"

Doug let out a whoosh of breath. "Word is Moreno's in Portland looking around. I didn't want to run into him with so many of my people out of town."

Sabrina went back to her room, but left the door open.

"So he's heading north to set up operations in Portland." Rafe shook his head. "A ramped up drug supply coming right at us."

"Looks that way. They're using more boats to move the drugs out of Mexico. Right up the coast. The feds are filling up the tunnels under the border as fast as they find them."

"So we get the honor of hosting Moreno and his thugs in our fair city." Rafe put as much sarcasm into his voice as he could.

"There's more. He's definitely after me and I'm a prime target of his vengeance. I wish I knew what form it would take, other than killing me himself."

"That could be his only goal."

"Look at us. Speculating on how I'll die."

Doug's expression changed to one of exasperation. "I have a feeling he's planning more than a quick execution. Why didn't he send an assassin long before this?"

"Do you really think it's because he wants to kill you himself?"

"I'm convinced he has more on his mind than just me. He wants me to suffer before I die. I'm afraid for everyone who knows me. Remember, he killed my wife."

"So you think Patti's death was not simply collateral damage?"

"I'm sure it wasn't. And those four years he spent in Mexico fueled his plans for revenge. He might target my daughters."

"If you can't find them, how can he?"

"I don't know. For years I didn't try to find them on purpose. Jenny said when she left me she feared for their lives and was taking them somewhere they'd be safe."

"And you think they may no longer be safe."

"Yeah. I'm going to have to find them before Moreno moves north. But Sabrina is our focus now. How's she doing?"

"She's upset, of course."

"She will get her daughter back. Once Nathan's in custody." He kept his voice low.

"Here? In Riley?"

"Yes. And I want to be in on the reunion. I'm a softy."

"Alison?"

Doug nodded.

"So we wait. And wonder what Nathan will try next." Rafe's

gut tightened. So much depended on the next hours, the next days. He glanced at the door to Sabrina's room. And what Sabrina wanted.

"WE SHOULD BE GETTING CLOSE," Nick said.

Rafe glanced at the GPS on his phone. "Looks like the next driveway."

"Pearson said it's a long one." Nick pulled in and followed the lane through a grove of cottonwood trees and stopped in front of a farmhouse with a wraparound veranda.

"No one will see us meet with Pearson way out here," Doug said. "Not even the same county. He's a smart man."

Pearson came out the front door. The four of them got out of the SUV and joined Pearson on the porch. "Let's sit out here," he said.

Rafe made the introductions, then sat on the bench seat. Sabrina chose a chair off to one side. She hadn't said anything since they left the diner after breakfast. Intimidated by three big men. And now four. He understood.

"I'm glad you could come." Pearson grinned. "I needed to see who I'm working with." He looked straight at Sabrina. "And I'm so sorry Nathan has caused you so much trouble."

Sabrina mumbled a thanks.

"Any sign of Nathan yet?" Nick asked.

"Near as I can tell, he picked up his dogs after leaving Pendergraf's office, then scooted out of town." Pearson brushed his hand across his eyes. "He's been in Riley all his life. I've only worked in Riley seven years. Before that, Tulsa, where I was raised." He gestured toward the trees out front. "A childhood friend inherited this spread when his dad died."

"And you can't let the chief know you're looking for Nathan." Doug frowned. "That puts us at a disadvantage."

"Yeah, it does. But my job's already in jeopardy. The chief is watching me closely." Pearson scrunched his brows. "Someone with the county might have tipped him off about the district attorney investigating him. And he suspects that I'm involved." His smug smile lit up his face. "Which I am."

Nick handed Pearson a manila envelope. "Here's the warrant for Nathan's arrest. We can prove the breaking and entering and destruction of property, but don't yet have the evidence for arson and attempted murder."

"Showing Nathan in possession of sodium fluoroacetate should be enough for most juries." That smug smile of Pearson's again. "Nathan made a mistake last night. He took the whole bottle out of the shed on my friend's property. It's missing this morning."

"So Nathan hasn't left the area," Doug said. "He's planning something else, something deadly."

Rafe glanced at Sabrina, at her sober, wide-eyed expression.

CHAPTER 25

Sabrina twisted her hands and shifted on the metal folding chair. They were in the newer part of the cemetery, where the headstones were flat, embedded in the grass. The scent of the fresh cut grass drifted her way. Towering oaks provided some shade from the mid-morning sun, though the air was crisp.

Granny's casket, draped with a floral blanket, sat on a bier, directly in front of Sabrina. The minister droned on.

She couldn't concentrate on what he was saying. What was Nathan doing? Her stomach churned and she gulped big breaths to keep her meager breakfast down.

No one had seen Nathan since he left the lawyer's office two days ago.

Sabrina's chest tightened. She should have felt safe, but she didn't. Even with Rafe seated on her left and Doug on her right. And Nick and Mike Pearson standing at the rear of the crowd.

The people gathered for her grandmother's funeral were mostly strangers. Only a few she recognized from childhood.

Mrs. Murphy had greeted her earlier, hugged her again and wished her well. She'd be heading back to the store as soon as the service was over.

Pearson told them when they arrived that Pendergraf wasn't there. Neither was Mr. Hornsby. Or Chief Howard. That bit of news had helped Sabrina's nerves. She doubted Dr. Atkins had bothered to come either.

The minister ended the service with a prayer. Then nodded at Sabrina. That was her cue to approach the casket to pay her respects. She stood on wobbly legs. Rafe gripped her elbow and walked the few steps with her and she placed her hands on the blanket of flowers. Letting her finger tips dig into the petals. Looking for solace that wasn't there.

What would it have been like to grow up here and know her grandmother all these years? Sabrina only had memories of Granny's neglect. Nathan's torment. No joy.

Sadness engulfed her. But the tears stayed away. She'd cried for Granny at the nursing home. She wouldn't cry for her own losses.

Sabrina moved off to one side of the rows of chairs where she could greet the mourners after they filed past the casket. The grave site was close to one edge of the cemetery, near a high hedge that blocked the view from the road. They'd walked a considerable distance from where the vehicles were parked. She longed to be back inside the SUV, heading to the motel. Then heading back to Portland. Away from Riley.

She couldn't help feeling edgy. She couldn't explain it, so kept it to herself.

Rafe and Doug moved back to give her more room as the townspeople expressed their condolences. She repeated, "Thank you for coming," many times in reply to their "I'm sorry for your loss." It all sounded so empty. So wrong. She was the one who'd stayed away for fifteen years.

A young dark-haired woman who'd been hanging back shyly approached Sabrina and introduced herself as Lisa Weigel.

"I love the jewelry you're wearing. Very distinctive," Lisa said.

Sabrina smiled. She always like to talk about jewelry. "I made them." She let her own pride show through in her words.

"Those are amethyst, aren't they?"

"Yes. My favorite gemstone. I use it a lot in the pieces I make."

"Do you sell them?"

"I had a shop where I made them and sold them. The interior was destroyed, but I'm going to rebuild."

She glanced at Rafe. He was in a huddle with Doug and Nick, about six feet away. But he was talking while also watching her. A ripple of awareness sped through her, even though she knew it was his job to keep an eye on her at all times.

Someone shouted. Then two dogs raced across the grass a short distance from the grave. A big black one and a smaller brown one. Both barking and growling.

"Nathan's dogs." Rafe rushed to Sabrina's side.

The people remaining ran for their cars out on the street.

The black dog turned and headed straight toward Sabrina. Rafe pulled off his jacket, stepped in front of her, and used it as a shield.

Sabrina backed up, almost to the hedge. Lisa grabbed her arm. "I'll protect you. The dogs know me."

The brown dog turned and headed their way too. Nick and Pearson in pursuit.

Doug had moved away, behind the casket. His cane would

be no match for snarling dogs.

Lisa pulled on Sabrina's arm. "That black dog is dangerous. He bites." She steered Sabrina to the end of the hedge. "We'll be safe behind here."

"No." Sabrina tried to pull away but Lisa gripped her arm tight. Then shoved her around the end of the hedge.

And there was Nathan. Her heart seized.

"Gotcha now." He grabbed her and before she could scream, he jammed a foul smelling cloth against her nose and mouth. She struggled and tried to kick him. Her legs were heavy. Wouldn't move. He laughed and held on to her. She pushed at him. Fought him with her remaining strength. Then slipped into darkness.

THE BLACK DOG snarled and charged at Rafe. He braced himself, his heart pounding. Then he tossed his jacket over the dog's head, hanging on, wrestling him to the ground. He wasn't sure his strength would be enough, but he immobilized the dog and kept him on the ground. All the funeral goers, including the minister, had quickly cleared out.

"Where's Sabrina?" Doug yelled.

"Damn." Rafe glanced where he'd last seen her. "She was by that hedge, with that other woman." He clung to the growling dog. "I can't let go of this damn dog. He'll bite me or someone else."

Doug limped over to the hedge and looked around it. "No one here. But a road where someone could have parked. "I heard a car rev up and take off. That woman. Who was she?"

"Lisa Weigel, Nathan's girlfriend," Pearson said.

Pearson held onto the brown dog. "Nick. Hang on to this

guy." Nick grabbed the brown dog and Pearson went back to his car. He got out muzzles and heavy leashes and secured the brown dog. Then he helped Rafe get the black dog leashed and muzzled. They tethered the dogs to trees. "No dog control in this town. The police have to do double duty when dogs need rounding up. I'll call an officer to come get them."

Rafe picked up his jacket. The dog had torn holes in it. He threw it in a trash can. Then he checked behind the hedge. "I smell chloroform. How do we find Lisa Weigel? She was the last person to talk to Sabrina."

"She's the daughter of a friend of mine," Pearson said. "The one with the poison." He took out his cell phone and made a call.

"Hey, Tim. Where is Lisa living? And what's her cell phone number?" He took out a pad and wrote on it. "Get a hold of her if you can. She's in big trouble. She may have helped Nathan kidnap his cousin. The cousin is in big danger. I need your help. Call me back if you find her." He ended the call.

He turned back to Rafe. "She lives in an apartment in Tracy, over the county line."

"Is there a county sheriff who can help?" Rafe asked.

"I'll notify them once we're on the way."

"How far is Tracy? Let's check there first," Nick said.

"And Nathan's house too." Doug limped to a chair and sat. "We'd better split up."

Pearson made three copies of her address and phone number and gave them to Rafe, Nick, and Doug. Then called an officer to pick up the dogs. "I'll try her phone now." He punched in the number. "Voice mail. I expected that."

"Wait a minute," Rafe said. "When we were here before, Mrs. Murphy said that Nathan bought a shack on a lake, for fishing."

"I hadn't heard about a shack," Pearson said.

219

"I'll go ask Mrs. Murphy if she knows how to find the place. Why don't you go check Nathan's house and Lisa's apartment?"

"I'll go with you to the store." Doug stood and braced himself with his cane.

"Are you okay?" Rafe gazed at Doug. He was favoring his right leg.

"Yeah. Just had to move too fast to get out of the way of the dogs."

"Come on, Nick. You're with me." Pearson started across the grass. "We can leave the dogs for the officer."

Rafe and Doug followed at a slower pace.

Rafe glanced back at the hedge. "Damn. I should have been ready for some kind of trick."

"Don't beat yourself up. He outsmarted all of us." Doug's words were quiet. "You had to stop that dog."

Rafe drove straight to the grocery store.

"I'll wait in the car," Doug said. "I've slowed you down enough."

Mrs. Murphy was alone at the cash register.

"Hi, Mrs. Murphy. Rafe Campbell again. I have a question for you."

"Oh, I remember you. Where's Sabrina?"

He frowned. "Gone. We think Nathan kidnapped her from the cemetery. Do you know how to find that shack of his?"

"Oh, I've been there, with my late husband. When it was owned by a friend of his. Good largemouth bass in the lake."

"Can you give me directions?" He took out a pad and pen.

"Follow the main road out of town to the south," she said.

Then she gave him detailed instructions on where to turn and how far. Even how rough that last lane would be.

He wrote it all down. "Thanks."

He burst out of the store in a run.

CHAPTER 26

*S*abrina moaned and tried to turn over. She couldn't. Her eyes drifted open. And her heart seized into a hard knot. A sour smell teased her nose. She lay on a narrow cot with a bare, filthy mattress. Not even a pillow for her aching head. Her hands were tied behind her, putting a strain on her shoulders and keeping her from lying flat. Her feet were tied too, with a thin rope. She tugged at her hands, but the rope only tightened, cutting into her wrists.

Nathan stood across the room, in front of a small table, his back to her. She was in the main room of what looked like a crude shack. Made of rough boards and very dirty. A big rat dug through the trash stuffed in the corner. Sabrina shuddered and looked away. Rats had roamed through the homeless camp where she'd lived in Seattle.

Her eyes slowly closed, blocking out Nathan, blocking out the room. Whatever he'd used to knock her out was still affecting her.

Another smell drifted her way. Hamburger and French fries? Her stomach growled. Breakfast was long ago.

Why am I still alive? She couldn't help wondering. He meant for her to wake up, since she was tied. What was he going to do with her? And why was she smelling hamburgers? Poison. He took the whole bottle from Pearson's barn. He was going to feed her a poisoned hamburger. He wanted to watch her die in agony.

Had anything she'd tried worked with him in the past? He liked for her to grovel. To beg. That wouldn't work now. She had challenged him in the lawyer's office. And he knew she had help. Maybe Rafe would find her before it was too late. Somehow she knew he would come. She only hoped she was alive when he burst through that door. She forced her eyes open again.

"You're awake. Finally." He growled the words in his meanest tone.

She remembered how it used to scare her. Now it was corny. An act. "These ropes are tight. Can't you loosen them?"

"I'll make them tighter if you don't stop complaining." He stood over her, his ice blue eyes boring into her.

She breathed slowly, trying to get her heart rate down. She had to keep her wits about her and not let fear take over and make her do stupid things.

"Now I can do anything to you I want." He jabbed a finger into her cheek until it felt like a bruise was forming. Then his eyes raked down her body.

She pulled herself into a tight ball. Like she was going to ward off any other blows. He laughed. And reached out and pulled her upright. Pain shot through her shoulders. She moaned. She'd been tied too long. Her wrists throbbed.

"What are you going to do? Did you bring me here to kill me?" She challenged him, though her voice shook.

He laughed, that cruel demented laugh she remembered from her childhood. He was enjoying this.

He turned back to the table behind him and picked up two hamburgers and set them on a box about three feet from her. Then set a bag of French fries next to each hamburger. The wrapper on one hamburger had been disturbed. The other wrapper was smooth, like it had come from a drive-through. Was there poison in that hamburger with the crinkled wrapper? Would he force her to eat it?

He sat on the cot next to her and untied her hands. She shook her hands and her arms to try to work some circulation back into them. He laughed again. That wicked laugh.

"What do you hope to get? There's no money left?"

"Revenge. You've been a problem for too many years." He used his normal taunting tone that had always grated on her. "Granny used to throw you up to me as perfect. Ask me why I couldn't be quiet like you."

"And you fell for that." She laughed. "That's what she said about you. That you were perfect and I was no good."

"She said that?"

"Yes. Don't you get it? She played games with us. Her own power trip." An image of Granny in that bed drifted into her mind. Had she been a lonely old woman for years? Sabrina was glad she was able to forgive Granny. Make her own peace with her. Her only regret now was not seeing her daughter again. Or Rafe.

Unless she could outwit Nathan.

"You walked right into my trap. I knew you would come, to see how much money you'd get." He sneered at her.

"If you kill me, you'll go to prison."

"No I won't." He laughed again. "I'm out of here as soon as you're dead. I don't have any reason to stay in Riley. I'll leave town and no one will find me."

"The detectives will. They're really sharp men."

"Then why haven't they caught me yet?"

"They will. Believe me."

"You're mighty sure of yourself now, aren't you? But that's not going to keep you alive. I'm still going to kill you before I leave." He stared at her as if he was trying to figure out who she was.

She'd said what was on her mind. She hadn't fooled him. He knew she was different and not the same person he'd bullied when they were young.

He unwrapped both of the hamburgers and put them on top of their wrappers. The one with the wrinkled wrapper was closest to her.

"Go ahead. Eat. Aren't you hungry? Doesn't that smell good?" His taunting tone was back. "I'll let you have a last meal before I kill you."

Sabrina's mouth watered. She was hungry. She glanced at him. At that smirk on his face. Would he force the hamburger into her mouth if she didn't bite into it willingly?

The rat in the corner ran across the middle of the room. Nathan picked up a piece of wood from the floor and threw it at the rat. Sabrina reached for the hamburger that had been in the undisturbed wrapper. And shoved the other one over.

She bit into the hamburger in her hand. The meat lodged in her throat and she started choking. She coughed and tried to dislodge the piece of meat. A reflex action. She'd taken too big a bite.

He laughed and watched her a minute as she choked and coughed. Then he picked up the other hamburger and took a big bite. Then another. She slowed her breathing, trying to stop the cough that wracked her body. She couldn't talk.

Nathan choked, then coughed. His eyes bulged with stark terror. He dropped his hamburger on the floor, then fell back onto the cot. She stood as best she could and shuffled out of his way. Then threw her hamburger into the corner where the rat had been in the trash. She stopped long enough to pull the rope off her ankles. Nathan writhed on the cot, moaning, his eyes shut.

She ran to the door, unbolted it, and slammed the door behind her. And ran out into the cleared parking area in front of the shack.

She was breathing hard and still had that choking sensation in her own throat. Surely her hamburger wasn't poisoned too. He'd obviously intended to eat that one without the poison.

She gazed at all the trees, at the lake out behind the shack. Trees grew almost to the edge. Who could find her out here? She'd have to start walking and hope someone came along who could help her.

After a glance at the front door that remained closed, she followed a path around the shack, to the edge of the lake. A small dock was tethered to spikes on the shore. She scanned the shoreline. No other cabins. No one here who could help her.

RAFE SLOWED DOWN THE SUV. He'd gone two miles on this paved road. The unmarked lane was just ahead.

"Is that it?" Doug leaned forward, pointing at two large oaks.

"Has to be." Rafe turned between the oaks and sped down a rutted road, through dense trees, going as fast as he dared. Doug hung onto the overhead support. "Don't get us killed."

Rafe didn't slow down. And Doug kept quiet. Sabrina was on both their minds. Would they get there in time?

Pearson had called ten minutes earlier. His friend found Lisa, but she swore she didn't know Nathan had planned to kill Sabrina, only that he was planning to kidnap her and take her to the cabin. Nathan told her it was because of money Sabrina owed him. Lies of course.

Rafe careened around a curve and almost lost control of the vehicle. He slowed down as much as he dared.

A clearing appeared straight ahead. Rafe gunned the engine and barreled into the graveled area in front of the shack. The door was closed. Nathan's car sat to one side. He jumped from the SUV. Doug opened his door and used his cane to stabilize himself on the gravel.

Then he saw her. Walking up a path at the side of the shack.

Rafe ran to her and crushed her to him, holding her close. Tears formed behind his eyes and he didn't try to stop them. "Damn. You had me scared. I thought he'd killed you."

She looked up at him. "He tried. But I think he's dying. He ate the wrong hamburger."

"I'll check inside." Doug went up the steps to the porch, then pushed open the door and limped in.

She looked so guilty. "It's not your fault," Rafe said.

"I was supposed to eat the other hamburger. I took the wrong one when a rat distracted him. I didn't know for sure that one was poisoned. I just suspected it, because the wrapper was crinkled, like it had been opened." She rushed the words.

"It's not your fault," Rafe said again. "He put the poison in the hamburger. Not you."

"I didn't want to die. I didn't trust him. So I grabbed the wrong hamburger."

"No, you grabbed the right one."

"Then I choked on the meat. I thought I was dying. He was laughing when he picked up the other hamburger and took a big bite." More rushed words, trying to get it all out. She was distraught.

Doug came out the door and stood on the porch. "He's dead. He put the poison in the hamburger. His fault, not yours. Believe it."

Sirens sounded in the distance. "I called 911 on our way here," Doug said. "We didn't know what we'd find."

The paramedics and ambulance arrived, followed by a sheriff's deputy in a cruiser.

The deputy got out. "What happened here?"

"You're going to need a medical examiner." Doug descended the steps slowly. "Nathan Prescott is dead."

Rafe held onto Sabrina while the paramedics and the deputy went inside the shack.

The deputy came back out, followed by the paramedics. He showed them his ID. "I work this end of the county. Who are you people and what happened here."

He looked at Sabrina and frowned. "Are you the woman who was kidnapped from the cemetery in Riley? I heard a bulletin earlier."

She nodded and mumbled a yes, but stayed in Rafe's arms.

Doug introduced himself and gave the deputy a quick rundown of what had happened and why. Including the information about the poison used and why Nathan was dead instead of Sabrina. Then he introduced Rafe as an employee of his.

Doug glared at Rafe, but he didn't let go of Sabrina. He'd come so close to losing her.

Pearson's official car roared into the clearing and he and Nick jumped out.

"Mike, what are you doing here?" the deputy demanded.

"I've been helping these folks, since the chief wouldn't." He introduced Nick to the deputy.

Nick spied Sabrina in Rafe's arms. "Sabrina, are you okay?"

She nodded again. Still not speaking since the others had arrived.

A medic approached. "I saw ropes inside. Are those rope burns on your wrists?"

"Yes. They hurt." She mumbled the words.

He went to his vehicle and came back with salve and gauze. Rafe had to let her go so the medic could attend to her raw wrists.

The deputy addressed the whole group. "As soon as the medical examiner gets here to take over the scene, I want all of you to come to the Sheriff's office." He glanced at his watch. "I'll call in some other deputies and order pizza. This is going to be a long evening. Lots of unanswered questions here."

CHAPTER 27

Sabrina yawned as she got out of the SUV in front of the diner. It was after midnight before they'd gotten to the motel for a short night's sleep.

She went through the door first, followed by Rafe, Doug, and Nick. The smell of bacon awakened her senses and lifted her spirits. They were all meeting for breakfast before the long drive north to Oklahoma City and a flight home to Portland. She couldn't wait to get home. To start rebuilding her business. To start making money. To start supporting herself again.

A pang of guilt hit her. Nathan had to die. Otherwise he would have killed her. But that didn't make her part in his death hurt less.

Rafe steered her to the big booth in the corner. She glanced back. Doug had stopped by the door and was looking down at his phone. It dinged like a text coming in. He smiled and followed them to the table, Nick right behind him.

Pearson came through the door and stopped Doug just short of the table. "Wanted to let you know. Pendergraf has been arrested. Embezzlement. And not just from Mrs. Walters' trust fund. More than one victim."

He looked at Sabrina and smiled. "There may be some money for you once he's convicted, or if he confesses. He was building himself a nice nest egg for retirement."

Her chest tightened. An inheritance. "Thank you for letting me know."

"Join us, Mike," Doug said." We're celebrating this morning. And you played a big part in this whole business."

"I'd love to. I admire the relationship you have with your people, Doug. You must be a great man to work for."

"Thanks. And if you ever want to get out of police work and come to Portland, there's a place for you in the agency. I mean that sincerely."

"I'll keep that in mind." Pearson scooted into the booth.

When they were all seated, Doug turned to Sabrina. "What else would you like, besides the money coming to you, to make your life complete?"

"Get my daughter back." She said it quickly. And hopefully. That's what her life needed now. Her daughter to make it complete. She glanced at Rafe, sitting beside her. She'd like him too. She'd finally come to her senses and realized she didn't want to live without him, but he might not want a ready-made family. Or even a wife.

"Here she comes." Doug stood.

Alison ushered a teenage girl in the door.

Sabrina's heart clenched. She was speechless. She was looking at a younger version of herself. Long brown hair and all. Just a couple inches shorter.

Rafe moved out of her way so she could slide out of the booth.

The girl walked right into her arms. "Momma. Is it

really you?"

"Oh, my. My Gracie. My little darling." She was babbling, but she didn't care. The tears started flowing unchecked. She couldn't have held back the flood if she'd tried. She'd longed for this to happen so many times.

"I changed my name back. I want to be Gracie for you." She was crying too.

They held onto each other and sobbed. Alison handed each of them several tissues. She'd come prepared.

When they'd finally dried their tears and stepped away from each other, Sabrina looked at Gracie and almost burst into tears again. "It's been so long. You were three days old when they took you away from me."

"I'm back with you, if you want me now." Gracie's expression was wary.

"Oh, yes, I want you. I never wanted to let you go. They stole you away. And sold you."

"Her new birth certificate says she's Gracie Ann Walters," Doug said. "She was Ann in her other life."

"It's okay, isn't it, if I keep the Ann name too?" Her question showed hesitation.

"Of course it's all right." Sabrina's smile was wobbly. "I want you to be comfortable with who you are. Now that you're back where you belong, with me."

Alison had stepped back out of the way. Sabrina reached for her and gave her a hug. "Thank you for bringing Gracie to me."

"Glad I could help." She was crying too. Sabrina glanced around. There wasn't a dry eye at the table.

They all settled into the booth. Now Sabrina knew why they'd sat in the big booth. She smiled at Doug. He'd planned this all along. She adored him. He was so thoughtful and giving.

Gracie sat between her and Rafe. Sabrina felt the separation from Rafe growing. She didn't want that to happen, but it was surely possible. They hadn't made any plans for a future together. No promises. In fact she'd said she wanted to build a life with her daughter. And now that Gracie was back with her, she didn't know how Rafe fit in. Or if he did.

THE STREET WAS dark and deserted when Rafe drove his own SUV down the familiar street he'd lived on for five years. He had two house guests now. Sabrina and Gracie. And it felt right. He wished he knew how Sabrina felt about it. With Gracie around, it might be difficult to have a serious talk with Sabrina.

He pulled into the parking space in front of the house. Behind his work car. Once he was inside the house, he disarmed the alarm. He went back outside and retrieved their luggage and brought it into the living room. He and Sabrina had traveled light and didn't have much. And Gracie didn't have much either. She'd been in foster care. He hoped Sabrina wouldn't mind shopping for her daughter. She'd hated shopping for herself.

Gracie looked around. "This is your house, Rafe? You own it?" She sounded skeptical.

"Yes. I like the extra room that an apartment doesn't have."

"Then you have room for a family here." She was beaming.

"Yes, I do." He waited to see what other words of wisdom came out of her mouth. He'd been delighted at what a chatterbox she'd turned out to be. Always said what's on her mind. Even Sabrina was talking more. Especially since Nathan was no longer a threat.

"I've seen how you look at my mother. Are you going to be my dad? I need a dad too."

"Whoa. I haven't asked your mother yet."

"Are you going to?"

Sabrina was laughing. "Out of the mouth of babes."

"I was planning to. When I found out if that's what she wants."

"Why don't you ask me what I want?" Sabrina said. She moved into his arms.

"I was afraid I'd bungled my chances when I didn't protect you at the funeral." He pulled her closer, but not enough so that it would seem out of place to a teenager.

"It wasn't your fault that Nathan tricked us," Sabrina said. "He did, you know."

"Yes, but I should have expected it. I failed you when you needed me." He let the regret shine through his words.

"I'm still alive. You did not fail me. Nathan killed himself with his own stupidity. I see that now."

"I'm beginning to."

"Maybe it was karma and had to play out that way. He died. Not a pretty death, but one he deserved, I guess. All he wanted was easy money. Granny's money."

"How did you get so wise? I guess that's what I truly love about you. Your courage and your intelligence. You kept your cool and did what you had to do to survive. A skill you learned early in life, thanks to Nathan and all his viciousness." He smiled. "And I definitely love you."

Gracie smiled. "See you two do belong together. And we can be a family."

Sabrina smiled at Gracie then looked at him again. "You know what I love about you? You're kind and considerate, and gentle."

She looked at him solemnly and he tensed.

"And I do love you, Rafe. You've given me a chance for a life above mere survival."

"Time to stop talking. Gracie, turn your head. I need to kiss your mom."

She giggled and turned toward the blinds drawn across the windows in the back.

Rafe ducked his head down and kissed her thoroughly. She melted into his arms like she belonged there. He had to stop or he wouldn't be able to. She awakened a deep longing in him that no other woman ever had.

He raised his head. "You will marry me, won't you?" He managed to get the words out through labored breath.

Her breath was ragged too. "Yes."

"Goody!" Gracie shouted. She was beaming again.

"It's getting late," Rafe said. And realized what he wanted now, more than anything in the world. Sabrina in his bed again.

He picked up two suitcases and headed up the stairs.

SABRINA STOOD in the middle of Rafe's bedroom. Is this what she wanted for the rest of her life? She still had some doubts about how they'd make a family together. Her and Gracie and Rafe. Would it work?

"You're not sure yet, are you?" Rafe asked. "I can see it in your eyes. Come, sit. Let's talk." He sat on the edge of the bed, leaving plenty of room for her.

She sat at an angle, not right next to him. She wanted to watch his face." You're always thoughtful and kind and willing to put up with my quirks. I do love you. I think what I was searching for was family."

His expression was thoughtful. "You found family. You have Gracie back."

"And I found you. Are you over your guilt enough that we can go on from here?"

"Ah, so it's about me, not you?"

"I think so. You were worried about failing me. You didn't. I'm still alive. I was the one who took the chance and talked to that woman I didn't know."

"Nathan's girlfriend was arrested for helping him lure you away."

"I'm sorry she got caught up in his schemes. He was truly a bad man."

"And I'm sorry he had to die the way he did. But you did the right thing, protecting yourself. You used your survival skills to come out of that shack alive."

"Are you at all concerned about taking on a ready-made family?"

"Hey, we'll both learn together. You don't have any experience parenting either."

She laughed. "You're right. I only had her for three days before she was taken from me."

"She said she wants a dad. I'm ready to be that dad for her." His words held a sincerity she truly believed.

"And I'm ready to be a wife to you. I did say yes to your proposal." She laughed again.

"We'll rebuild the interior of your shop and you can go back to work, if that's what you want. We'll get Gracie enrolled in high school so she can finish out what's left of the school year. Doug said she was an honor student in Nebraska."

"I hadn't heard that. You know more than I do."

"You've been talking to Gracie. I've been talking to Doug.

Oh, by the way. He gave us his blessing." He smiled, that sweet gentle smile she loved so much.

Somehow she'd moved closer and found herself in Rafe's arms. The warm protection of his body so close. And she felt safer than she had ever felt.

"And we can grow old together, right here if it suits us." Rafe tightened his hold on her.

"I like your house. It's a real home. I feel like I've come home."

"You have." And his mouth captured hers.

AUTHOR'S NOTE

Thank you for buying Dare to Challenge! I hope you enjoyed it. This book is number two in the Those Who Dare series. All the books in this extended series are connected to Landreth Investigations in Portland, Oregon. Book three, Dare to Conquer, will be out soon. Watch my website for more details.

http://barbararaerobinson.com

You can also subscribe to my newsletter on any page of my website and receive advance notice of future publications in the series or future books.

ABOUT THE AUTHOR

Barbara Rae Robinson writes romantic suspense novels that sizzle with the heart-pounding rush of danger and the edgy emotions of falling in love. After her debut romance with Harlequin, Barbara turned her attention to combining romance with suspense. Her current project is an ongoing series of tales of death-defying heroic men and courageous women. Barbara lives in rural Oregon, close to Portland, the setting of her current series.

http://barbararaerobinson.com

facebook.com/barbararae.robinson

twitter.com/Barb_Robinson